The Luck of the Ogre

by

Annette Miller

Garland Falls

The Luck of the Ogre

Cover Art by *Tina Lynn Stout*

The Wild Rose Press, Inc.
PO Box 708
Adams Basin, NY 14410-0708
Visit us at www.thewildrosepress.com

Publishing History
First Edition, 2026
Trade Paperback Print ISBN 978-1-5092-6432-2
Digital ISBN 978-1-5092-6433-9

Garland Falls
Published in the United States of America

Dedication

For my sons, Scot and Alex, who made me believe in my dreams. And for my husband, Brian, who now walks with real angels.

Prologue

Wayne tapped the invitation for his friend Renee's anniversary party against his knuckles. He couldn't believe a whole year had gone by since he was in Garland Falls for her wedding. After the fight on the Halloween before with a large, supernatural entity, not a lot scared him anymore. And the invitation had come at the right time. He'd just been dumped by another woman. Maybe his ogre side was messing with his leprechaun luck.

Renee and her husband were spirit conduits. While his accounting job at a prestigious firm was based more in the "real" world, he carried the potential for some serious magic of his own. Odd balls of light would appear and then disappear when he turned to them. He watched as a rainbow flowed through the paper in his hand. Okay, this had to be from his leprechaun heritage. That and the gold coins showing up in his pockets all the time. Well, that wasn't so bad, but it happened more frequently the closer the calendar got to St. Patrick's Day.

He'd made his reservations at Warner's Bed and Breakfast in Garland Falls, Minnesota, for two weeks. He'd be back in Trenton, New Jersey, and ready to get to work as soon as he returned. He looked forward to catching up with Renee and her husband. The small mantel clock chimed midnight, and he yawned. PJ's on, teeth brushed, and now time to get some rest. As soon as sleep claimed him, the same dream started again.

He stood on a riverbank and watched as a boat approached. A person covered in a heavy cloak poled the boat to the shore. As it got closer, fog swirled around his ankles, and he smiled as he waited. He climbed aboard and sat while the boatman pushed back out to the middle of the river. Skeletal hands grasped the pole, and the figure turned its hidden gaze to him.

The person lowered the hood, and a skeleton stared at him.

He'd gotten used to the bony appearance of the person in front of him. At least he didn't want to scream any longer. "It's nice to see you again. I think. You aren't here to take me to some land of the dead, right?"

"No, of course not. I mean you no harm." The female voice swirled as soft as the waves slapping the boat. "Please, don't fear me. I have searched for you."

"I'm not afraid of you, but I am curious. Who are you?" He leaned forward, folding his hands as his arms rested on his thighs. "Why search for me? I have no ties to wherever this place is."

"You have more ties to this land, and others, than you realize." Her hollow eye sockets burned into him. "Wayne Billings, you must come to Garland Falls. Your safety depends on it."

"I've already decided to take a trip out there. Who am I in danger from this time?"

She chuckled, her voice like wind in the trees as it faded away. "There are tribes who have started to fight over who gets to claim you. Don't worry. Your friends can help you, and I'll be there to protect you. Look to the sky."

As he did, a rainbow appeared to stretch down to

circle him. "Do you know why a rainbow keeps following me or coming around me? Does it have something to do with my leprechaun lineage?"

"It means you have more power than you ever dreamed possible."

The dream came to a quick end, and Wayne rubbed his eyes. He'd been having this dream ever since the rainbow appeared and the calendar turned to March. What did it mean? Of course the skeleton woman would have ties to the small town in the middle of nowhere Minnesota. He sighed and fell back. Stranger occurrences had happened to him in Garland Falls.

One way or another, he'd have an interesting trip.

Chapter One

Dee Warner scampered around the large mahogany check-in desk and grabbed Wayne in a tight hug. "Wayne Billings, how wonderful to see you again. Your hair's gotten darker since Renee and Parker's wedding. I'm so happy you came. The party will be so much brighter with you here."

The lobby of the B and B hadn't changed at all. The mahogany check-in desk was a beautiful complement to the light hardwood floors. The furniture in the dining room off to his right matched the mahogany staircase. The small table by the door held a large crystal vase and overflowed with green-and-white carnations with an occasional yellow mum poking up from the center.

The short older woman held him in a hug tight enough to crush his bones. Dee Warner hadn't changed a bit. She'd tucked a white carnation with green along the edges into her silver hair. She wore a pale-yellow blouse with green slacks and a white vest. Her blue eyes still held the joyful sparkle he'd come to admire.

"Hi, Miss Dee." He smiled as he hugged her back. "It's great to see you again. Warner's Bed and Breakfast is still one of the most beautiful places I've been." He winked at the older lady. "You do know I only accepted Renee's invitation because of your wonderful cinnamon rolls, right?"

She patted his shoulder and chuckled. "You old

charmer. Yes, I knew you'd want some and have a fresh batch ready to come out of the oven any minute now."

"The decorations in town for the St. Patrick's Day festival are every bit as impressive as I knew they'd be. Looks like Mrs. Hall had her legions work overtime for the event. Every store has decorations in the windows, and the banners on Main Street add a nice touch."

Dee's eyes twinkled with delight. "Make sure you let Adelaide know. As much as she brushes off the praise, I think she enjoys all the compliments. Of course, she denies it when I or anyone else tell her so." She stared at Wayne for a few more heartbeats. "I think this celebration will be very important to you."

"Then I guess I'm glad I decided to stay until after St. Patrick's Day."

He looked around. Besides the table by the door, Dee had vases filled with yellow, green, and white carnations on almost every surface. Small leprechaun statues had been placed on the check-in desk, and he knew for a fact more would be in the rooms. All the items related to St. Patrick's Day gave him a sense of peace. The more he saw, the more warmth filled him, and he began to feel like he belonged here. "It's strange, but your B and B feels like home to me now."

She gave him one final squeeze. "I'm happy you feel comfortable at Warner's. It's always a pleasure to have you here."

"But I've only been here twice before. The first time at Halloween, then last year when I came back for Renee's wedding."

"Oh, pish tosh. Those two visits count more than you think."

The front door banged open as Renee Callahan

threw herself at him. "Wayne!"

He staggered back and struggled to keep his balance.

She squeezed him around his waist. "I'm so happy you decided to attend. The party wouldn't be the same without one of our best friends here. Parker got so excited when your reply came to say you'd be here to help us celebrate."

His friend hadn't changed either, except for the happiness that radiated from her. Her shoulder-length, auburn hair had grown a little, and she hadn't put on much weight, still as trim as ever. Her green eyes shone with delight as she held him. She was the perfect balm to his, once again, broken heart.

He held her hand as they walked out to the porch. "To tell you the truth, I was glad to get the invite. Things haven't gone so great back home."

She frowned a little. "Oh? I hope no nasty entities followed you to cause you more problems." She gazed down the hill to Main Street. "Garland Falls has been pretty quiet for the last several months. We even had some new people move to town."

"You said that the last time we talked. My problems can wait, and they aren't too serious. At least, not serious enough to put a damper on the party. The worst is my latest girlfriend broke up with me. It was probably for the best." He gave her a sudden smile. "Where is Parker anyway? I thought he'd be in here with you."

She shook her head and gave out an exaggerated sigh. "He still has work to do to get ready for this weekend. How long can you stay?"

"Two weeks. I have plenty of vacation time. I wanted to have some time to spend with you and Parker. I also want to get to know Garland Falls a little better.

My reservation is through St. Patrick's Day."

"Why St. Patrick's Day? You picked a pretty specific time."

"I don't know." He glanced around the property before sitting in one of the rockers. "There's a feeling I have to be here until then. When I saw the town's decorations and the figures and flowers Miss Dee put out, it all calms me somehow. The closer St. Patrick's Day gets, the more I feel a pull of something. I'm not sure what it could be, but I think it might be my leprechaun magic waking up."

"It's a strong possibility. You did demonstrate some pretty sweet moves against the Huntsman before. That had to be your ogre side coming out."

"I also have this dream where I meet a skeleton woman. I'm not afraid of her, and sometimes I think I already know her."

She sat next to him. "Oh?"

"It starts at a riverbank when this boat comes up. She's poling the boat and tells me I have to come to Garland Falls. I could be in danger from who knows how many different factions. She also said she can protect me. You have any thoughts about this?"

Renee sat back and rocked with a pensive expression. "Except for the woman, it sounds like Charon. He takes souls to the underworld." She looked at him. "But you aren't dead, and maybe she has an important message for you."

"I hope the message isn't I'm about to die." He chuckled and sagged back in the rocker. "I don't think I'd like to find that out anytime soon."

"I've never heard of Charon, or his subordinates, giving advance notice of death to souls. Maybe you should talk to Miss Dee or Mrs. Hall about it. They may have a better explanation than I can give you."

"I'd love to know why I can't get my love life straightened out." He shook his head before he glanced at her. "Here's something else strange, but not bad or terrifying. Coins appear in my pockets by themselves, and a rainbow follows me wherever I go. Sometimes it's bright, and sometimes it dims a little."

She laughed. "I'm sure your luck will change for the better sooner rather than later. Maybe this woman in your dream will show you the way." She glanced up at the sky. "There's no rainbow up there right now."

"You can't see it?" He turned to her when she shook her head. "Trust me. It's up there, and it appeared on your invitation also."

"It might be linked to your leprechaun heritage. Leprechauns and rainbows are pretty inseparable. It's possible you might find a pot of gold or some other treasure at the end."

"You could be right." He rocked for several minutes and didn't speak. "I wish I knew what it all meant. Renee, you know me. I've always been logical to the point of stubborn. I'm confused how I feel about this magical pull inside me. As for the skeleton woman, sometimes I think I see her as flesh and blood. I like her, and somehow, I think she likes me, too." They sat in silence for several minutes before Wayne shook his head. "So where is this shindig anyhow?"

She reached over to take his hand and gave him a small nod. "Here. Miss Dee let us set up in the backyard. Parker did a great job with the gardens back there, and his brother added a few extra touches to the gazebo."

"Can we take a look?"

She stood and pulled him to his feet. "Sure. I've been back there several times already. I know Parker will be happy to see you."

They walked to the back of the B and B. A small army had set up tables, chairs, and hung decorations. A large wooden square covered part of the ground for dancing later when the band would play. Mrs. Hall stood in the middle and commanded everyone in her usual fashion. This had gone from a small party to a serious grand affair. Of course, with Mrs. Hall in charge, a huge party was the only outcome.

Wayne watched them for a few minutes. Parker hadn't changed much either. His tawny hair still reached his collar, and his height made the stout little lady at his side appear even shorter than he remembered. When Parker turned, his hair had plastered itself to his forehead from the hard work he'd done.

Parker and Mrs. Hall glanced in Wayne's direction and hurried over.

"Glad you could make it," Parker said.

Mrs. Hall threw her arms around him and held him tight. "Renee got so excited when she found out you decided to attend."

Wayne squeezed the older woman and smiled at Renee. "She's my best friend. I couldn't disappoint her. I love how you have the town all decorated for St. Patrick's Day. You amaze me every time, Mrs. Hall. Garland Falls is lucky to have you in charge of all these festivals."

"Oh, you stop with all your nonsense." Mrs. Hall's cheeks turned pink, and she glanced away. "I love what I do, and it shows."

Parker gestured to the yard and all the setup in

progress. "What do you think?"

"It all looks fantastic." Wayne winked at Mrs. Hall. "I can see why you want this lady in charge. I'd like to take a walk to see the whole setup, if you don't mind."

"Go ahead and poke around. I'd like to hear what you think. See you in a bit."

Wayne gazed at the people who worked on final touches as he wandered. He couldn't believe the anniversary party had gotten so huge. A small shed at the back of the yard caught his eye, and he frowned. The party décor and tables weren't anywhere near it. He walked over and laid his hand on the doorknob. Dark-purple color surged through the door, and he snatched his hand back.

An electric shock had zinged through him, and the fine hairs on his arms stood straight up. He rubbed his fingers together and stared at them. Did he hear faint voices bleed through from the other side? Okay, no people were in there, and he didn't hear any voices. He'd keep his distance from the shed and the odd feelings it gave him.

As he hurried back to the others, he glanced over his shoulder. He half expected the door to open and a horrible creature to storm out. He shook his head and rolled his eyes. Now he'd let completely ridiculous thoughts into his mind. He would scare the heck out of himself for no reason if he wasn't careful.

Renee smiled at him when he got back to her side. "So will this be a great party or what?"

"I believe it will be the best party ever. I think it will put every other party to shame." He put his arm around her shoulders and gave her a quick squeeze. "And I've been to a lot of parties."

"You always know just what to say." She checked the time on her cell phone. "I've got to run into town and get a few more supplies."

"Give me your list, and I'll go. The past couple of times I've been here, I didn't get to see too much of the town. Running a few errands should help me out with a little bit of sightseeing."

He hesitated before leaving. He turned to her as she texted him what she needed. "Renee, what's in the little building at the edge of the yard?"

"Parker keeps his work tools in there. Why?"

"I just need to ask him about it. Something strange happened, and I want to make sure it really happened or if I'm crazy."

"I'm sure he'll be able to help you with whatever you need to know. Now get going. I need those items."

He pulled up her text with the list as he walked to his car. He hesitated before grabbing the door handle and tugging it open. No purple, no voices, no weird electric zings running through his hand. He sighed and drove down to Main Street. Renee's list wasn't too long, and he wouldn't take too much time to get everything she'd asked for. He hurried into the general store, picked up what was needed, and stowed them in the back seat.

He glanced around, and his gaze came to a complete halt on the little bookstore across the street. "Keyes' Imaginations," he murmured. "Love the name. I can take a few minutes to go in."

Chapter Two

"Hi. Welcome to Keyes' Imaginations."

Wayne stared at the woman behind the counter. Her long, black hair had been pulled up into a ponytail, and she held an armload of books. She seemed familiar, like he'd known her all his life.

Her bright-blue eyes shone with laughter as she came around the counter. "Are you okay?"

He shook his head. "Yes, thank you. I'm all right. We haven't met before, have we?"

She laughed, the musical sound filling his heart with joy. "I don't think so. I'm Eleanor Keyes. Welcome to my store. What brings you in today?"

Her voice sounded familiar, though he couldn't quite place it. Had he met her before, like at Renee's wedding? Anything was possible in Garland Falls. He'd found that out the hard way eighteen months earlier, but he refused to dwell on the past. He shook off the weird déjà vu and smiled. Her voice reminded him of the skeleton woman from his dreams. But Eleanor stood in front of him, flesh and blood. Not an exposed bone anywhere.

"I'm Wayne Billings. I ran some errands for my friend, Renee Callahan. I'm in town for her anniversary party." He glanced around the shop. "I saw your place and couldn't resist coming inside to check it out."

"I'm glad you stopped in, then. Books do have a

magical pull for people, some more than others. I know Renee very well. Her shop is across the street from mine, and we often have lunch together."

He grinned. "Then I guess you'll be at Renee and Parker's party?"

"I wouldn't miss it. I hope you'll save me a dance or two."

"Maybe even more than two." He checked the time on his phone. "It's getting late. I should go back to Miss Dee's. It was nice meeting you, Eleanor."

"Nice to meet you, too, Wayne."

He stood there and gazed at her. Why couldn't he make his feet move toward the door? The bookstore had more than just books pulling him in. Eleanor gazed at him while he stood there. Warmth zigzagged through him, making his blood race in his veins. He wiped his sweaty palms on his pants. Eleanor made him nervous? He never got nervous around new people or women. Well, there was a first time for everything.

"Thanks again for talking with me. I'll see you at the party." Wayne wiped his hands on his pants again. "I suppose I should get going. Bye, Eleanor."

He drove back to the B and B, Eleanor occupying all his thoughts. He knew they'd never met, so why was she so familiar to him? And did he want to know her more? That was an easy question to answer. Yes. He wanted to get to know Eleanor Keyes very well indeed. After all, any woman who tied his stomach into knots and gave him sweaty palms had to be more special than anyone he'd ever met before.

****

Wayne spotted Parker and Renee and waved. "How's it going back here?"

13

"I think we're done for today," Parker said as Wayne approached, carrying the bag of items. "There's a few minor details left to take care of, and we'll be ready for guests."

Wayne gave him a thumbs-up. "That's great to hear."

Renee wrapped her arm around Parker's waist. "Wayne has a couple of questions for you."

Wayne glanced at the grass when Parker turned his attention to him.

"Head on home." Parker kissed the top of her head. "Wayne and I will talk."

"See you at the house." She grinned at them as she took the bag from Wayne's hands. "Don't talk until the sun comes up tomorrow."

Parker rolled his eyes. "Won't happen."

As Renee left, Wayne looked at Parker. "Still a man of few words, aren't you?"

"Yep." He led Wayne to the gazebo and sat on the bench. "How can I help?"

"When I checked out the setup earlier, I saw the small shed at the back of the property. When I touched the doorknob, the door turned purple and I thought I heard voices. It also gave me a pretty sharp electric shock. She said the shed is where you keep your tools, but I think it has another purpose. She told me to talk to you about it."

Parker sat quiet for a few minutes and thumped his fist on his leg. "She's kind of right. I do keep supplies in there for my work."

"And what else?" Wayne said when Parker didn't continue.

"The purple door is one of the entrances to the Dark

Lands." Parker stood and paced through the small area. "It shouldn't have reacted to your touch, not without the key needed to open it."

Wayne stood silent for a moment, then held his hand up. "Stop for a second. What's the Dark Lands?"

"Sorry. I forgot you're still pretty new to all this." He took a deep breath and continued, "The Dark Lands are where some evil fairies—and some other not quite as evil creatures—live. They aren't bad, but they aren't good either. Since half of you is an ogre, half of your heritage is in the Dark Lands."

"Great. So now I'm evil?"

"I don't think so. You're also half leprechaun, and they're from the Light Side."

Wayne flopped down on the bench. "So if I can't say I'm good or evil, what the heck am I? Do you think it's why a skeleton woman has started to talk to me in my dreams?"

Parker stared at him. "What skeleton woman?"

"I've seen her multiple times. She doesn't scare me, but I do feel like I know her. She tells me some people are after me, though I guess I shouldn't be surprised. A rainbow also appears, and I'm the only person here who can see it. And check this out." He reached into his pocket and pulled out a gold coin. "Random money appears in my pockets. You have any thoughts about the weirdness around me this time? I mean, your wedding didn't have any threats, and we took care of the big one on Halloween."

"Your skeleton woman sounds like the daughter of the Ferryman. I didn't think she could contact mortals through dreams, though." Parker sat across from him and folded his hands, resting his arms on his legs. "I wish I had answers for you." He suddenly stood and walked out of the gazebo to stare at the sky. "Nope, no rainbow."

"I guess it's because I've got leprechaun blood. After all, you never see one without the other." When Parker held his hand out, Wayne gave him the coin. "You know what this is?"

"This is leprechaun gold. Look at the marks."

Wayne stared at the coin, wondering why he'd never taken time to study it before now. One side had a four-leaf clover etched into it. The other side held a stylized letter L in old script. The edges were smooth without the usual grooves found on contemporary coins. He glanced at Parker and saw his concern reflected in the eyes of his friend.

"I think you may have to travel to the fairy lands. I'll have Lucas secure an invitation for you into the Dark Lands so you'll be prepared. You'll have to make a visit to the Light Side to figure out your leprechaun abilities." He paused to glance at the sky and rubbed his thumb over the coin. "I've never heard of leprechauns who see rainbows or manifest coins."

"I don't think you've ever said so much to me or anyone." He smiled as Parker frowned at him. "Just a joke, buddy. Thanks for your help. I'm not sure I want to go to the Dark Lands. It sounds a little out of my comfort zone. It'd be nice if I could contact the skeleton woman here in Garland Falls. Traveling to the fairy world sounds a tad risky."

They walked back to the front of the house.

"I'm sure you'll find your information here. You may even be able to find out who's after you on your own. Still think you need to talk to the leprechaun colony to get your other answers."

Wayne watched Parker get into his truck and drive away. He was more certain than ever he'd be making a trip to the fairy realms. Not exactly how he wanted to spend his time here. He'd heard the concern in his friend's voice as he talked about the Dark Lands. If Wayne's leprechaun luck cooperated, he'd get all his answers without ever leaving the bed-and-breakfast. He headed up the stairs to get some rest.

****

Wayne lay on the bed in the same room he'd had before. The pale-blue walls matched the comforter. A small desk and chair were set near the window. Gauzy blue curtains did their best to hide the night from the cheery room. Miss Dee had also placed a vase with pale-blue roses on the dresser. The light scent filled the space and calmed his heart. The questions burning in his mind settled down, and he thought he might actually sleep through the night.

Miss Dee had given him a huge dinner and topped it off with her delicious cinnamon rolls. Even though the night air turned chilly, he'd opened a window a crack to listen to the night sounds. A person didn't get this kind of gentle quiet in the city.

"You know something, Renee?" he murmured to the night. "I finally get why you love it here so much. To tell you the truth, I could get used to it myself."

Maybe he could open an accounting office, pick up some clients. He shook his head, turned over, and yanked up the covers. He had a great job back east and made the kind of money a lot of people dreamed about. He'd just made partner at his firm also. He couldn't give up what he'd built to move to a tiny town in the middle of Minnesota. He closed his eyes tightly and held the covers in a firm grip. Could he?

Once again, the boat pulled up to the shore, and he got on. He stared at the figure, and he grinned. She was a skeleton, but something about her called to him. He could almost swear she was beautiful in her own, bony way.

She pushed out onto the silent river and turned her eyeless gaze to him. "Tell me, Wayne Billings. Have you come to Garland Falls and found out who wants to claim you?"

He shook his head. "Not yet but I made it to town without any problems. I did speak with Parker Callahan. He told me you sound like the daughter of the Ferryman. So are you his daughter, and have you come to Garland Falls for me?"

Her sightless gaze bored into him. "It's quite possible you could find me there."

"Are you the Ferryman's daughter?" he insisted. He hated to repeat himself, but she'd avoided his question. "I have to know."

She laughed, a deep, throaty, musical sound. Odd when she had no lungs or organs for it to sound so full of life. "Congratulations. You've discovered my heritage."

He smiled and raised an eyebrow. "I don't have to die to meet you, do I?"

"Of course not. If so, you would've found your way here by yourself. You wouldn't have needed me to meet you in your dreams. My father frowns on dream speak. He says it confuses mortals too much."

"I guess you know about my parentage." He leaned forward, still smiling at her. "I feel like I've already met you in Garland Falls. Are you there?"

She pulled the pole into the boat as it bumped against the shore. "I show up in Garland Falls on occasion. We'll meet soon now that you've arrived. It's possible we've already met." She waved her hand in front of his face. "Return now to the mortal world."

Wayne opened his eyes and folded his hands behind his head. He'd had a conversation, a real conversation with the Ferryman's daughter. She'd said it was possible they'd already met. He thought about all the people he'd met so far. The only one who sort of matched her was Eleanor Keyes. Impatience made it hard to sleep, but from wanting to meet the skeleton or wanting to see Eleanor again? He'd figure it out when the time was right and not before.

Chapter Three

Wayne still had one more day before the party. He decided to drive down the hill and check out Main Street again. He hadn't paid too much attention to the stores when he'd run Renee's errands for her. His gaze was drawn immediately to the bookstore. His heart hammered as he saw Eleanor helping customers through her large front window.

He wanted to run right over and talk to her again, but would that make him look desperate or, worse, pathetic? Renee's shop beckoned to him, and he forced himself to cross the street. The blue-and-gold letters painted on the window sparkled in the morning light. The window display of bags, belts, and small purses invited customers to come in and look around. The bell chimed over the door, and she looked up from the back of the store.

Bright sunlight highlighted small dust motes floating in the air. The pungent odor of new leather filled his senses. He recognized the scent of oil she'd used to rub her leather products to make them waterproof. All the familiar sights and the remembered scents of her work took him back to the first time they'd met.

"Hi, Wayne." She stood and wiped her hands on a cloth as she came around the counter. "It's nice to see you in town on such a beautiful day."

Her greeting took him out of his reverie. "Your party

isn't until tomorrow, and I didn't get to see much of the town when I was here the other day. I did stop in the bookstore, though. It's a nice place, and there's a lot of stock in there." He gazed around her shop. "Your place here looks better than the one you had back east."

"Isn't it amazing?" She stood in the middle of the floor and spread her arms wide. "Parker and his brother set up the whole store for me when I went back to close my other shop and to take care of selling Gran's house."

He nodded and smiled. "I think the Callahan boys do good work. I know you sent me pictures, but I have to say they didn't do the place justice." He walked over to one of the glass cases and looked inside. A small bag with books on it grabbed his attention. "This is really nice."

What could be special about this item? Renee had done beautiful work with the stitching and the bead design. He shook his head and stood back. As he did, another gold coin fell out of his pocket. He handed it to Renee. "Here. You can keep this. The way these coins multiply, I don't think I'll ever run out. I'll let you get back to work. I wanted to pop in and see you."

She reached into the case and took out the small bag. "Here. You gave me a coin, so you basically paid for this. Give it to someone special."

"I will."

He put the bag into his car and continued to meander down the street. General store, cookie shop, hardware store, the diner, and almost at the end stood Wilkerson's Garage. At the very end of the street was the town hall with the library right next door. All in all, a neat little layout. He turned and walked the other way. More stores and at the other end of Main Street stood the school, a modest-sized hospital, and a small church.

He chuckled. In a town of magic, they still had a church. He wondered what kind of services they held. Would they be what he would find in churches back east, or were they of the more magical kind? Didn't matter either way. He'd never been one to go to church. Still, knowing people here had comfort when they needed it was nice.

The bookstore claimed his attention even when he tried hard to concentrate on window-shopping. Keyes' Imaginations had a magical pull on him, like the woman who sold books. He wanted to give himself and Eleanor a little more time before he went back to her store. Deep in his heart, he could almost feel her wanting him to come back. With the way his love-life luck ran, taking things slow and easy struck him as the better path to tread.

He'd started to think Garland Falls could be a nice place to live. He wandered down the street and hated the fact his father had been given such a hard time when he lived here. When the truth about his mother's death had come out, the town elders had tripped over themselves apologizing and trying to make up for past mistakes. He'd taken a long time to forgive them for their early prejudice, but Renee had let him talk it out until he understood.

He paused in front of the general store and glanced back at the bookstore again. Maybe the Ferryman's daughter had a good reason to talk to him almost every night. Maybe she wanted him to make a connection with Eleanor. Maybe she had a message from his parents. Maybe he should stop overthinking and realize it might be a simple, easy explanation. Simple would be nice for a change. He had enough regular-world problems without adding magical ones to the mix.

He stood and stared at the bookstore. He clamped down on the urge to go over there and spend all day with Eleanor. It might be okay to go in and say hello. Before he changed his mind, he trotted across the street.

"Hi, Eleanor."

Her smile brightened, making his own grow wider.

The knot in his stomach loosened. Looked like he'd made the right call. "I wondered if you needed a ride to Renee and Parker's party tomorrow."

"No, I've got transportation, but it's nice of you to ask." She walked around the counter. "I'm glad you came in. I found something for you." She handed him a book of fairy tales. "I don't know why, but I thought you'd like to read this."

He opened the book and carefully turned the pages. "This edition is really old. It's got to be worth a small fortune." He looked up and smiled at her. "How did you know I still like fairy tales, even as an adult?"

She shrugged. "I still like them, and something told me we have that in common." She closed his hands on the book and left them there. "This was mine when I was little."

"Thank you. It means a lot you would trust me with something so special." His hands tingled where her fingers rested on them. Maybe Eleanor was the one for him and that's why relationships never worked out in New Jersey. "I'll return the book when I finish it."

"There's no rush." The bell chimed over the door. "As you can tell, there's no rest for the wicked or the bookseller. I'll see you at the party."

Wayne walked out, holding the book to his chest. A

sweet snack would go perfectly while he read the tales he could almost recite from heart. He spied the cookie shop Renee had fallen in love with and headed that way.

As soon as he pushed open the door to the Heavenly Bites cookie shop, he inhaled deeply. He held his breath for a moment, then let it out a little at a time. The smell of bakeries always took him back to when he and his dad would go to one after a day out. Vanilla, coconut, almonds, chocolate, sugar, and various other scents flowed around him and soothed his frazzled nerves.

A woman with short dark hair came out from the back and smiled. "Hi. Welcome to Heavenly Bites. What can I get you?"

He peered into the case. "How about a chocolate chip and a macaroon? They both look great."

She reached into the case and grabbed the ones he'd ordered. "You must be Renee and Parker's friend. The one who came here on Halloween about a year and a half ago. You were also here for their wedding. I'm Joanna."

"I'm Wayne." He shook her hand. "Renee told me after she found your shop, she would never, ever leave Garland Falls."

"She does come in a lot." She turned as a tall man with long white-blond hair came out, a baby in his arms. "This is my husband, Davin, and our son, Marcus."

"Nice to meet you." Wayne let the baby grab his finger. "Hey, little guy. Have all three of you planned to come to Renee and Parker's party on Saturday?"

She nodded. "We wouldn't miss it."

He pulled out his wallet. "What do I owe you?"

Davin shook his head. "Not one dime. It's a welcome gift. I hope you'll come back before you have to leave town."

"I'd say it's a strong possibility."

Wayne walked out and took a deep breath. Even the air here had a special kind of a tang to it. He glanced back in at the couple who waved to him. He waved back and continued down the street. Garland Falls was special in more ways than one, and warmth from the sidewalk rose up and curled around him. He smiled as he thought maybe the little town wanted him to stay here after all.

Chapter Four

The day of the party arrived. Wayne took extra care with his appearance. He wanted to make a good impression for Renee and Parker's family and friends. He brushed his brown hair back, again pleased with his decision to stop getting highlights. Garland Falls had been an influence, even when he'd gone back to the city. His appearance wasn't nearly as polished or "fake" as it used to be.

He turned his head left, then right. "Still, I think I should have gotten a haircut before I left. I certainly can't meet clients looking like this."

He tugged on a light-green pullover shirt and left the buttons open. Tan khaki pants and his brown loafers made him look dressed up, but not too dressed up. At last, he felt ready to meet Renee and Parker's friends and guests. He glanced at the book of fairy tales and covered a yawn. He never should have stayed up so late reading.

He walked to the window and pushed the gauzy curtain aside. Not a cloud in the bright, blue sky, but the rainbow still arced over the town. He peered closer at it. The end of the rainbow looked like it stopped at the B and B. He grinned and dropped the curtain. As he walked to the door, a familiar jingle in his pocket caused him to hesitate. He reached in and pulled out more coins.

He headed downstairs as the gold coins weighed his pocket down again. He held up his hand and swore he saw the rainbow light flow through his fingers. He pulled out one of the coins, and the light surrounded it before the color faded away.

"I used to be so grounded in reality." He shook his head as he continued down the steps. "I thought it'd be harder to get used to the fairy world and magic." He held up the leprechaun gold again. "I have to admit it—I was wrong."

He walked into the dining room, and as soon as he sat, Dee came out with a plate and set it in front of him. Questions churned in his brain, and he wanted to ask them but didn't know how to start. Could Miss Dee see the rainbow? Could she have a clue about how the coins appeared in his pocket? Those answers would have to wait for another day.

"Most of my other guests have already left. I saved you a light meal because there's enough food out there for a week. My niece made some wonderful pastries to add to the table."

Wayne grinned. "It sounds like I'll go back east at least ten pounds heavier than when I came."

Dee laughed and patted his shoulder. "You might. As soon as you finish, go on outside. Guests started to arrive as soon as the sun rose."

He hurried through his breakfast and walked outside. Miss Dee was right. The backyard teemed with people as they milled around. At the center of the crowd stood Renee and Parker. She looked like she enjoyed all the attention while he looked like he wanted to run and hide. Wayne knew Parker, with his quiet nature, would never be the social type.

Renee walked over to him and introduced him to the crowd. He smiled and nodded, thankful again for his business luck. He could always remember names and faces, an important ability in his field. At the back of the crowd, he caught a flash of jet-black hair.

He turned to Renee. "Who's the woman back there, the one with the black hair?"

She took his hand. "She's a friend of mine. Come on. I'll introduce you to her." They hurried over, and Renee smiled. "Eleanor, I'd like you to meet my friend, Wayne Billings. He took time off from his job to come to our party. Wayne, I'd like you to meet Eleanor Keyes."

Eleanor held her hand out. "We meet again, Wayne."

"Yes, we do. I wanted to start reading the book you gave me right away, but I got sidetracked by cookies." He narrowed his eyes as he stared at her. "I still feel like I know you from somewhere."

Eleanor's eyes sparkled with humor as she smiled at him. "Hopefully, it will come to you. I know how frustrating those kinds of thoughts can be."

"Maybe we should spend some more time together. You know, to help it come to me."

She laughed her musical laugh again. "I think you just handed me one of the most original pickup lines I've ever heard."

"I've been told I do have a way with women." He glanced down, and his cheeks flamed when he realized he still held her hand. He let go and stepped back. "Sorry. I didn't mean to keep your hand prisoner."

She chuckled a little. "I didn't mind. I should go talk to some more people. I look forward to having at least one of the dances you promised me. I also want to see you at the store before you leave."

"Same here." He watched her walk away and the easy way she talked with the crowd around her. "She sure didn't stay with me very long. And here I thought leprechauns were supposed to be lucky," he mumbled as he joined the crowd. "I think I might be the unluckiest leprechaun ever born."

As Parker approached, he tried for a neutral expression and wasn't sure he succeeded by the way his friend was looking at him. *I'll just ignore the fact I look like a lovesick schoolboy, and maybe he will, too.* "Hey, Parker. You and your brother outdid yourselves. I've never seen so many flowers in one small yard. This is beautiful."

"Mrs. Hall had a lot to do with it, too." He stared at Wayne, then shrugged before nodding toward the stout, older lady as she oversaw the food layouts. "She insists she be involved in every event or party in Garland Falls."

"I've been told this on numerous occasions." Wayne grabbed a glass of punch from the table next to him. "You have to admit she's good at what she does."

"Hey, Parker."

They both turned at the sound of his name. Parker's brother, Lucas, trotted across the yard and waved at them. The brothers were almost identical in their looks. They were both tall and had tawny hair, but Parker had hazel eyes while Lucas' eyes were green. They both had strong arms from working with plants. Where Parker didn't talk much, Lucas talked a lot.

A tall woman followed behind him.

"Hey, guys. Blair got back in time for the festivities." Lucas took the woman's hand. "Blair, this is Renee's friend Wayne Billings."

As she shook his hand, he stared at her. Her pointed

ears showed her elven heritage, but her blue eyes and black hair stopped him in his tracks. "Nice to meet you. You remind me of someone I just met."

Blair tilted her head a little and studied him. "Really? I work with the HSA and only got back about an hour ago."

"The what?"

She smiled. "The Holiday Security Agency. I work there to keep supernatural creatures in line when they decide to get out of hand. You aren't a troublemaker, are you?"

"Oh. No, I'm not a troublemaker. I came in from New Jersey for the party. I'm an accountant." He shrugged as he glanced in Eleanor's direction. "You resemble Renee's friend Eleanor Keyes. That must be who you remind me of."

Lucas laid his hand on Wayne's shoulder. "He's an okay guy, Blair. He helped with the Huntsman."

"When I heard how you helped defeat that supernatural pain, the whole agency breathed a sigh of relief. You were a great asset in the fight." She waved toward the crowd. "I want to say hi to Renee. Excuse me."

As she walked off, Lucas and Parker steered Wayne inside the gazebo.

"This is the most private place we'll get today," Lucas said. He reached into his pants pocket and pulled out a large key. "Parker told me you might need to go to the Dark Lands soon. I went through and got permission for you to be there."

Wayne took the key, surprised by its weight. "What's this for?"

"It's a return key." Lucas glanced at his brother.

"We had it made special for you. If you get lost and can't find your way back, use this key. If you put it in any keyhole, it will open the door to the shed here at the B and B." He gave him an ivory paper with thick black script. "This is your invitation. Show this to any guardian, and you'll be able to pass without a problem."

Wayne curled his fingers around the heavy, brass key and tucked the invitation into his pocket. "Thank you, guys. I appreciate this more than you'll know."

"Parker didn't say why you might need to make this trip, but let me tell you this. Eat before you go. If you eat the food in the Dark Lands, you could be trapped forever and the return key won't work. You're half Dark Lander, so I'm not sure if it will be a factor or not. Best not to take any chances." Lucas stepped back. "Can you tell me why you need to be there?"

Wayne glanced at each of the brothers. "I think the Ferryman's daughter has a message for me."

Lucas smiled as Parker nodded. "Then it would be unwise to ignore the summons."

"I met Renee's friend, Eleanor. She has the same features, the same hair, and the same eyes as your wife. They aren't related, are they?"

Lucas chuckled. "Not to my knowledge, but let's not ask her. Blair's sisters married into royalty back where she's from. I don't think Renee's friend has her lineage. We wouldn't want to send Blair off on a rant about her sisters and their stuck-up husbands."

"Agreed. Why take a chance on me looking bad to someone I just met?" Wayne stared at the crowd, which had grown larger by the minute. "Shall we join the party?"

The three men left the gazebo to talk with the guests

as the band warmed up. Wayne's gaze was drawn to Eleanor as she laughed with a group of women.

He walked over to her and held his hand out. "I saved you a dance, Eleanor."

She smiled and placed her hand in his. "Just one? I thought we talked about more than a single dance."

"As many as you like." He led her out to the dance floor. "We can dance all night if you like."

"Sounds like a wonderful idea."

The slow song ended and changed to another with the same mellow beat. Wayne glanced down at Eleanor as she smiled at him. "You're a great dancer."

"Thank you, Wayne." She moved a little closer and laid her hands on his shoulders. "I think it's because I'm with you. No other man has ever held me like you do."

He swallowed hard, not wanting to say something to make her walk away. "It's just…I think you're amazing."

"How would you know? We've only spoken a few times."

He pulled her closer and glanced at the rainbow flowing around them. "Let's call it a feeling I have."

As they swayed in time to the music, Eleanor fit into his arms and against his chest like she was made for him to hold. He wanted to hang on to this moment forever. How could a woman he'd met such a short time ago be the one who made him feel like his bad leprechaun luck would improve? Eleanor could be the treasure at the end of his rainbow.

As the thought hit him, the rainbow glowed brightly before settling down to its normal brilliance. He'd take that as a sign he was on the right track.

Chapter Five

The party didn't break up until well past midnight. Wayne dragged himself up to his room and sagged down on the bed. He pulled his shoes off and rubbed his feet. He'd danced most of the night away with Eleanor and smiled, remembering how she'd felt in his arms. They'd talked and laughed, and little stings of jealousy had stabbed his heart when another man asked her to dance. When he claimed her for the next dance, she'd smiled like she knew everything he felt.

After Renee had broken up with him, he hadn't found anyone to fill the void. Yes, his good luck held strong in his business life. He loved to work with money and numbers. No one was surprised when he'd become the youngest ever to make partner at the firm. He walked through the office and ignored the jealous stares stabbing his back.

However, he couldn't claim the same success in relationships. He hadn't thought he'd ever find someone special again, but then he'd met Eleanor. She had a quality about her he sensed on an unknown level. The way she fit in his arms, his ease with talking to her made him cautiously start to believe she might be the one for him. He couldn't wait to be with her again and ask if she felt the same.

"If I hadn't been such a self-absorbed jerk in the past, maybe my ogre half would leave my love life alone.

I can't believe how selfish I was back then." He looked up at the ceiling, a soft sigh escaping his lips. "You were so right about me, Renee. I'm glad you're happy now, and Parker's a decent guy. My happiness will come in time. I just hope it will be sooner rather than later."

He reached into his jacket and pulled out what the Callahan brothers had given him. The invitation had been written in fancy, old-fashioned script. The brass key looked too big to fit in any door. "Let me guess. This thing is actually a skeleton key. The irony is too much." He chuckled as he examined it in the low light from the table lamp. "Skeleton key, skeleton woman. You have to love it. I guess skeletons are a part of my life now."

He did and didn't want to go to the Dark Lands. Yes, he might get answers there, but what else would happen? Maybe he could get the reason why his life had turned more to his magical side. The skeleton woman filled his thoughts, and uncertainty made him squirm as he sat on the bed. He hoped he wouldn't have to go to the underworld to meet her. At least not for another few decades at least.

He hadn't had a chance to talk to Mrs. Hall or Miss Dee. They might be able to give him some advice about the strange dream and whatever his leprechaun powers would do next. He gripped the key tighter. Maybe he wouldn't need to go to the fairy worlds at all. Maybe, just maybe, Eleanor was the one he needed to get all of the minor inconveniences which popped up in his life to turn around.

He returned the key to his jacket pocket and made sure his pass to the Dark Lands was still there. Why would the Ferryman's daughter say he could be protected in Garland Falls? Would he still have to journey to the

Dark Lands if the problem could be resolved here?

He walked over to the window after getting ready for bed. "Garland Falls, you always seem to raise more questions than you answer. One of these days, you and I are going to have a long talk."

A breeze blew the curtains into his face, and he smiled. The town agreed with him. Well, as his dad used to say, *tomorrow is another day*. Answers would come when they wanted to.

****

Eleanor paced in her room. Her father had forbidden any more dream contact with Wayne, and she could understand his point. Of course, she did take delight in vexing her father at times, but he never stayed mad for long. Her mother made sure of that, being the peacemaker of the family.

"Why would the ogres want to bring Wayne to the Dark Lands?" she murmured. "I know they'll have some devious reason, but what could it be?" She paced the length of her room, trying hard to work out what she should do next. "I bet the leprechauns are planning something also."

She loved her home in the Dark Lands as much as she loved her bookstore in Garland Falls. Her room in her father's house rejuvenated her and made it easier for her to stay in the mortal world. She liked the mortal world and loved the customers in her store. She felt as much at home in Garland Falls as she did in the Dark Lands. Maybe she'd turn down the opportunity to be the next Ferryman. Her siblings could take up the position as easily as she could.

She walked to the window and stared out. The River of Souls flowed by in a strange, eerie, yet peaceful silence. The murky gray-green water barely rippled as it flowed in its endless journey. The river was the main path to carry the souls of the departed to where they would spend eternity. For most of her life, she'd craved this job and loved to watch the river.

"Mortals are so complicated, but then again, I guess the residents of the fairy lands aren't much better. My soul sight shows me more mortals are good than bad. I guess that's a small consolation, though." She folded her bony arms around where her stomach would be. "Fairies and mortals have more in common than either race realizes. And yet I choose to live in both worlds. I'm going to have to pick one world or the other eventually."

She'd wanted to get to know how mortals thought. She'd never thought life among them would give her so much joy. Now she had to decide how she wanted her future to play out. She'd always wanted to be a ferryman, like her father and all her ancestors. Now she had her bookstore and all the people in Garland Falls. She also had Wayne who she'd fallen for the moment she contacted him on the dream plane.

She sighed. "If my life is complicated and my thoughts are troubled, I've no one to blame but myself. Why Wayne Billings and why now? Do I have a deeper connection to him than I first realized?" She dragged her bony fingers across her skull. "These thoughts are giving me a headache, and that's not even possible for a skeleton."

Yes, she found mortals interesting, but she'd never had any attraction for denizens of the Dark Lands or the Light Side. Wayne's lineage lay in the fairy realm, but he lived in the mortal world. He'd be so much happier if he were with his own kind.

"But which kind will want to claim him? His ogre kin or his leprechaun kin? If I thought my skeletal life had complications, it doesn't compare to his problems." She sighed again and laid her skull against the glass. "Or my attraction to him which I feel grow day by day."

"I hear you talking to yourself," her father said behind her. "Do these troubled thoughts keep you from your rest?"

"Yes. They all want to get my attention at the same time." Eleanor walked over to him and wrapped her arms around him. "I'm worried about what the ogres have planned for Wayne. If the leprechauns jump on the 'grab Wayne' bandwagon, things would get more complicated than they are now. I'm so confused, Dad. I know he needs to be in Garland Falls, but I also think he needs to be with me."

"He could be the one for you. I know how much you enjoy your time as flesh and blood." The Ferryman squeezed her a final time before he let her go and stepped back. "Word has reached me of unrest in the ogre tribe and the leprechaun community. As the mortal holiday of St. Partick's Day approaches, Wayne will feel the pull to the Light Side lands even stronger. He may not be able to resist." He chuckled and tapped a bony finger against his chin. "I wonder how the ogres will react to his Light Side heritage."

"I'm pretty sure they won't like or tolerate it. One or both sides could want to claim him for their own. With his mixed heritage, he could have a lot more power than he thinks."

"I agree, and your mother has seen he will figure out what to do when the time is right." He laced her skeletal fingers through his. "This is why I have told you to stop the dream communication. Trouble can come from anywhere at any time."

"I know. You never know who could be listening. I like Wayne a lot, Dad."

She walked back over to the window, and her father followed and kept ahold of her hand.

"Do you think we would have a chance at happiness? I mean, I'm a skeleton. A real non-breathing skeleton. Sure, I'm a flesh-and-blood woman in the mortal world, but not here. I can't stay there all the time. The Dark Lands are my home." She was quiet for a moment. "But I really like being in the mortal world too."

He tilted her face up. "All you are, all you feel is real. Don't despair, Daughter. Your mother has seen a bright future for you. This Wayne fellow might be the answer to all the questions plaguing you. I'm sure he will like you as much as you like him."

"I hope so, Dad."

After he left, she crawled into bed. As a skeleton, she didn't need to sleep, but all creatures, living and undead, needed to take some rest to recover their strength. She still wondered how much rest she would get this night as Wayne filled her thoughts.

Chapter Six

Wayne blinked as sunlight splashed across his eyes. He yawned and stretched before he sat up on the side of the bed. Renee's anniversary party had worn him out a lot faster than the corporate functions he attended in the past. A glance at the clock showed the day had started to slip away. A visit to the bookstore to see Eleanor again took top priority on his to-do list.

He showered, came out of the bathroom, and rubbed his hair with one towel, another one wrapped around his waist. He reached out and touched the closet door, and the deep-purple color flowed through it again. He yanked his hand back and stared. Another electric zing sent tingles through his fingers and up his arm. The dark-purple color faded, and he frowned. He took a deep breath and touched the door again.

This time, when the door faded to purple, he twisted the knob and pulled it open. He saw a landscape of twisted, dark trees and an unnatural reddish-purple sky on the other side. The trees themselves were black with gray leaves, and thick underbrush tried its best to choke them out. Vines crawled up the trunks, and small creatures scurried sight unseen through the woods. Low voices were carried on the slight breeze and beckoned him to come through.

He slammed the door shut, closed his eyes, counted to ten, and opened it again. Inside, his suitcase and all his clothes sat undisturbed. He glanced toward the dresser. Maybe moving all his clothes there would be a good idea. He didn't want to be freaked out by a weird land every time he opened his closet to get dressed. Then again, Garland Falls could be considered home to the weird and unexplainable. He dressed and walked downstairs. Goose bumps covered his arms as he tried to ignore the memory of the low voices which insisted he come through. Before he got to the dining room, Parker and Miss Dee's voices drifted to him and his name came up.

"I'm worried about him, Miss Dee," Parker said. "If the time comes when he has to go to the Dark Lands, he won't know how to navigate the roads in there, if there are any roads left. Lucas said it looks worse every time he has to travel there. With the St. Patrick's Day festival right around the corner, everyone's too busy to instruct him on what to do."

"Pish tosh, Parker. He'll be fine. After all, he's been given an invitation."

"What if he runs into trouble? Lucas and I won't be able to help him. Too many Light Siders in the Dark Lands could cause a lot of unnecessary problems for both sides."

Wayne heard the clink of dishes and knew Miss Dee cleared the table while she talked. He stepped into the room and smiled at the two. "I'll be fine, Parker. It's nice of you to worry, though."

"You heard?"

Wayne nodded. "I have to say I did. Like Miss Dee said, I do have permission to be there. Trust me. I have no immediate plans to go to the Dark Lands." He sat at the table while Dee brought in a plate for him. "Even though events have taken a strange turn for me, I'd rather stay in Garland Falls. I hope I can find out what I need to know here. I'll go to the Dark Lands if I have no other choice."

"You look out of sorts." Parker sat across from him and smiled when Wayne raised an eyebrow. "Green Men can sense when situations aren't right. What's happened?"

"Twice now, when I've touched a door, it turned purple. My closet door did it, and I opened it. If what I saw is a part of the Dark Lands, you can rest assured I don't want to go there anytime soon."

"What did you see?"

Wayne ate his breakfast while the pair waited for him to speak again. "A land with black, twisted trees and a reddish-purple sky. I heard animals in the underbrush, but I couldn't see them. I swear I heard voices, and they wanted me to come through. I'm pretty sure I don't want to know what lives there. It didn't look like a nice place at all."

"It can be a harsh land to visit." Miss Dee picked up his dishes and laid a fresh cinnamon roll on a small plate in front of him. "Some of the residents are evil, but some aren't. However, none of them care for visitors either."

"You confirmed what I said earlier." Wayne broke off a small piece of the roll and ate it. "I'd rather avoid a trip to the Dark Lands altogether."

Dee sat next to Wayne and patted his hand. "You're a very wise man. Only the foolish wish to go when they feel it might be dangerous."

"Dangerous? Who or what is over there?"

She sat quiet for a moment. "The Dark Lands are hard to describe. I've had some interactions with people from there. Some are okay and others, not so much. All have tempers, paranoia, and bad attitudes."

She cleared away the dishes, and Wayne muttered, "You didn't answer my question."

Parker stood, and Wayne followed him when he finished his breakfast.

"Head to Main Street today and explore for a bit." He clapped Wayne on the shoulder. "Try not to open too many doors. Especially if they turn colors."

"I'll do my best."

Wayne walked over to his car and hesitated as he reached out to the car door. He breathed a sigh of relief when it didn't turn purple. Did doors in houses open to different lands or any door he tried to open? Would other doors turn the same purple, or would they be different colors? Once again, Garland Falls' main commodity seemed to be questions with no answers.

He parked in front of Renee's store and got out. He stared at the bookstore and wanted to go over immediately, but would he look desperate if he did? He'd do a thorough search of the stores here first, then casually make his way over. He waved at Renee through the window and continued down to Mac's General Store. He took a deep breath, waiting, before he laid his hand on the knob to push the door open. Merchandise lined the walls to the left and the right. Not a weird sky or spooky tree to be seen.

His shoulders sagged, and his breathing steadied as he explored the goods on both sides of the aisles. The salty, buttery scent of popcorn flowed around him from the stand in the middle of the candy counter. He saw more variety of items here than in any of the stores back east. The aisles went back farther than he thought.

Garden and lawn equipment were propped up in an alcove at the back.

Steps to his left went down to another level, and he wondered what he'd find down there. Could be toys, could be clothes, could be almost any product he could name. Mac looked like he tried to carry everything ever produced. General store indeed. He couldn't get more general than all the different items around him. However, the man in charge couldn't be found.

"Hello?"

"I'll be right out," a voice called from a short hallway.

Wayne grabbed a few items and added them to the handbasket he'd picked up near the front counter. He didn't need to buy any necessities, but he'd been captivated by some small trinkets and decided it wouldn't hurt to be frivolous once in a while.

Mac walked out, a handful of paperwork in a messy pile in his fist. "Sorry. I didn't hear you come in. The figures on these invoices don't want to come out right. I've tried all morning to make the numbers work, and they simply won't cooperate."

"I can help if you want." He held his hand out. "I'm Renee Callahan's friend, Wayne Billings. I'm an accountant. Would you like me to take a look?"

The older man held the stack out. "Looks like it's my lucky day. I'd be glad of any help you can give me." He narrowed his eyes as he stared at Wayne. "I remember you from Halloween around eighteen months ago. You helped with the Huntsman problem. I can't tell you how happy we all were you could lend a hand."

"Yes, sir. I was glad to help Renee and Parker." He paused, knowing what he needed to say, but he wasn't sure he should. "You might have heard about my parentage."

Mac nodded. "You're the one who's got leprechaun blood in him." When Wayne confirmed it, Mac burst out in a hearty laugh. "Then this is my lucky day. It's not every day a leprechaun happens to show up when someone needs them most." He leaned close with a conspiratorial wink. "Though the rumors say leprechauns do exactly that."

Wayne had to grin, Mac's good humor infecting him. "I think you might have something there."

****

Once again, his business luck kicked in. He'd always had the knack to find a client who needed him the most. Once more, the tiny thought tickled his brain maybe he could open an office here and do very well for himself.

"Garland Falls, you need to stop trying to convince me to stay here." He winced as a stronger nudge pushed against his mind. He rolled his shoulders, but the thought he could move here wouldn't dissipate, no matter how hard he tried to banish it. "I have a great job back east, and I'm pretty sure I'd like to go back there when my trip is over. And now I talk to the town like it can hear me. Oh brother."

Wayne walked back to Mac's office and spread the papers out. He'd seen neater bookkeeping from clients with receipts in shoeboxes. Still, he'd worked with worse. He set his cell phone on the desk and opened up the calculator. After two hours, he discovered the error, but he found a lot more than the main one. He had to wonder how any of the man's books came out right. He called Mac into the office.

"Your overhead is way too high, and your profits aren't where they should be." He pulled out a diagram he'd put together. "If you follow this plan and get yourself a computer with a decent bookkeeping program, you'll be able to keep better track of your expenses."

Mac stared at the plan Wayne had worked out. "Are you sure this will work?"

"Trust me. Leprechauns are good with money, and I'm no exception. You follow this plan, and you'll be fine."

"I think I'll hire you to help me with this stuff." Mac glanced up and grinned. "You know, you might be able to help a lot of the businesses here if you ask them."

Wayne raised an eyebrow. "And now you want to convince me to move to Garland Falls? You've joined a list of people telling me the same thing." He wanted to say he already had a job he loved, but the conviction wasn't there, and he couldn't get the words out. "Starting a business in a new place is hard."

"Maybe, maybe not. I'm sure you'll find your path if you stick around long enough."

Wayne paid for his items and walked out, puzzled by Mac's statement. How could staying in Garland Falls help him find his path? He already knew his path, didn't he? He gazed around the stores and smiled. It wouldn't be the worst idea, but his job, the city, and all his friends were in Trenton. If he counted the thoughts the town put in his head, he had two "people" who wanted him to put down permanent roots here.

"Hello."

He turned and saw Eleanor headed toward him loaded down with two overfilled tote bags. "Hi. Can I help you with those?"

"Thanks." She handed them to him and shook out her fingers. "Those bags got heavier by the minute. I'm on my way to open my shop."

He hefted the bags as he fell into step beside her. "I had wanted to come see you this morning, but I didn't want you to think I was a creepy weirdo. Aren't you a little late to open, though? Most of the other stores have been opened for about an hour."

She laughed. "Maybe, but the party didn't break up until the early hours, and I needed to sleep in a little. The town gives some slack on the day after a party, but this doesn't mean I shouldn't hurry." She squeezed his hand. "And I don't think you're creepy or weird."

He waited while she unlocked the door to the store and walked in with her. "Can I help you get ready for the day? Are there any jobs you need done? I mean, since you are running a little behind."

"If you would turn the closed sign to open, I'd appreciate it. I'll get the register ready."

She gave him a few more small tasks while she set the front counter for her customers. He watched her move around the store with an easy grace he never spied in anyone else. She felt so real, much more so than the people he met at his company's functions. He helped her shelve new books and grabbed a cloth and wiped down the shelves, the counter, and the display in the window.

"So how long have you had this store?" He had no desire to rush through the tasks she'd given him. Being near her made every improbable thought seem like the best idea. "You've got the whole new-store smell in here."

She turned a brilliant smile to him. "About five years. I don't do too bad, but I do better when it's tourist season. As for the 'new-store smell,' I use different aromatherapy scents to keep the air and the atmosphere fresh and welcoming."

"I get it." He pointed to the window. "You've done an amazing job here. It's comfortable, and it's not stuffy like a lot of stores I shop in at home."

"Thanks. I work hard to make people feel comfortable."

She took a handful of books down one aisle, and he followed her.

"My customers all say exactly what you said. They feel at home here." She looked around and smiled. "I want every person who comes in to know they are welcomed."

He gazed at her and took her hand after she put the books away. "You're a special lady, Eleanor Keyes. You made me feel welcome as soon as I met you."

"I'm glad. I also loved dancing with you at Renee's party."

They stood close together, not speaking, and Wayne leaned in a little. The door chimed as a customer walked in, breaking the spell around them.

"Excuse me for a few minutes."

Wayne watched her walk away, his thought turning to the kiss they'd almost shared. He wandered through the store, checking out titles he found interesting. A door near the back grabbed his attention, and he frowned. He stepped closer, checked to see if anyone stood near him, then grabbed the knob. It turned purple and opened again to the Dark Lands. He closed the door, opened it again, and it became a normal storage room with books and supplies on the shelves.

He stumbled back a few paces, his hands shaking

and sweat popping out on his forehead. The door hadn't changed the second time, but that didn't mean it wouldn't if he touched it again. If he did, would it open back up into the Dark Lands? He glanced toward Eleanor, and she still helped her one customer before more had come in.

Time to get to the bottom of this. He glared at the door, refusing to let something so mundane scare him. His hands turned clammy, and he ran them down his pants legs to try and dry them. As he grabbed the knob, the door turned a golden yellow. He yanked it open, and the land inside looked like it belonged in a fairy tale. Great. Now he had to deal with a whole different colored door and a whole new land.

Trees with bright-green leaves swayed in a soft breeze, and the scent of roses and other flowers drifted out. The golden sun shone bright in a cerulean sky as birds glided on the wind. He could hear music, soft and gentle, kind of a mix of classical and Celtic. Instead of the sharp zing the Dark Lands door gave him, light and warmth filled him. Again, he heard voices asking him to come through.

"I am not going to this land either. Yes, this place looks friendlier than the Dark Lands, but I don't trust the way it showed up." He noticed a rainbow arcing across the sky. He glanced out the window, and the rainbow here shone bright. "Two rainbows in two lands at the same time? Is my leprechaun lineage responsible for these? It would be great if someone other than me could see them."

He pushed the door closed and leaned his head against it. "What is going on here? I don't have these problems in my apartment." He thumped his head against the door. "Why here and why now? It might be because I'm in Garland Falls. It couldn't be St. Patrick's Day because none of this happened last year."

Garland Falls had to have jump-started whatever power he carried in him. Every time he thought his life couldn't get any stranger, some incident would prove him wrong. Coins jingled in his pocket, and he rolled his eyes. The rainbow in the sky appeared to arc right down to the top of Eleanor's store. He grinned as a strange thought struck him. Could this lovely lady be his "pot of gold" at the end of this rainbow? How nice if that were true.

Chapter Seven

Eleanor came up behind him and laid her hand on his shoulder. "Do you feel all right? You've been standing here for about ten minutes, and you were talking to yourself. You're also a little pale."

He rubbed his forehead and turned to her. "I'm fine. I guess I didn't eat as much as I thought I did at breakfast." He straightened up and rolled his shoulders. He didn't want to mention the door, the rainbow, or the magical coins. "Tell me more about you. I mean, you know I'm an accountant from Trenton, New Jersey. I like numbers, and I'm good with them. What made you want to open this place?"

She looked around her store and laid her hand on some of the books. "I've always loved to read, and I ended up with so many books my parents told me I could open my own store. I love to share stories with my customers. I could talk about books all day." She walked him over to a spot at the back of the store. "These are all used books from my own collection. The rest of the store is filled with the newer titles."

Wayne walked over and stared at the shelves. "You've got a great variety here. I've read a lot of these." He peered closer at a couple before he took them down and thumbed through them. "I think I'll buy these."

She took the books and read the titles. "*The History of Leprechauns* and *Tales of the Ogre Tribes*. Odd books for an accountant to pick up."

"Everybody has to have a hobby."

He followed her to the front and paid for the books. She handed him a tote bag to put the books and his purchase from Mac's inside. He hesitated, then blurted out, "Can I buy you lunch today? I'd like to get to know you more."

"Sure. I'd like to get to know you more also. Come back around one. Sal's Diner should be done with most of the afternoon crowd by then."

"I'll see you then." He turned to go, then stopped. "I'll be right back." He hurried out to his car, grabbed the tote bag he'd purchased from Renee, then rushed back into the store. "I bought this for you the other day."

Eleanor took the bag and studied it. "I saw this in Renee's store and had thought about buying it for myself." She clutched the bag to her chest before running around the counter to grab him in a tight hug. "Thank you so much, Wayne. I love it."

"You're welcome. I knew it was you the moment I saw it." He gazed at her for a moment. He had other errands to run but couldn't make his feet move. "It's strange, but I don't want to leave. I also can't believe I said that out loud. I suppose I should let you get back to work. I'll be back at one."

He forced himself to step outside and turned. She still watched him, and he lifted his hand and waved. A different zing ran through him when she smiled and waved back. He'd only met her the day before at the party, and yet he found he craved her attention. Her smile made joy bubble through his veins. Happiness hadn't zoomed through him this much in ages.

He stuffed his hands into his pockets to hold the

coins, and he whistled as he walked away. Why did Eleanor and Garland Falls make him so happy? This little town had a way of melting most of his normal stress away. He rolled his eyes. Yes, but then replaced it with weirder stress. Like a rainbow no one could see but him. He glanced at the sky. The same rainbow flowed through the puffy, white clouds, following him like a colorful puppy.

He headed toward the town hall and the little park behind the building. Maybe reading one of the books he'd bought would help pass the time. Having more knowledge of his heritage might help. Movies weren't the best sources of information about ogres or leprechauns. He got through the first few pages about the ogre tribes before his mind wandered.

Why did the doors here react to his touch? Why were they two different colors? The gold and purple had to be connected to his parentage. He carried both dark and light inside him. Did the doors open because people over there wanted him to come to them? What would happen if he didn't want to go? Did the Dark Landers plot revenge on people they didn't know? He rubbed his eyes and leaned on the picnic table. If he had any idea how to broach the subject, he had plenty of people to ask.

Leaves rustled behind him as branches snapped in two. He slowly got to his feet as he tried to see through the woods around him. A large shadow loomed just inside the tree line. Whoever or whatever he faced had better have good answers for why it skulked about in the shadows. He'd been intimidated by creatures here before, but not this time. This time things would be different.

"Who are you?" He frowned at how deep his voice

sounded. "What do you want?"

"I've come to deliver a message from your people. You need to come back to your tribe." A low voice held a hint of menace and echoed around him. "Your chief demands your presence, and you will do as you are bid."

Wayne glared at whoever stood there, his hands balled into fists as his arms shook. "I have no chief, and I refuse to go anywhere with you. I don't know who or what you are, but you need to go back where you came from."

Wayne rubbed the back of his neck as nausea crawled from his stomach to burn his throat. Why would this person or whatever make him ill? His legs trembled, and he swallowed hard to keep his breakfast down. What about this creature nauseated him badly enough to make him want to run for the nearest trash can? He suspected who he talked to, and instead of fear filling him, only anger burned in his veins.

"Let me guess. You're an ogre, and you're here to make me go with you." Wayne folded his arms and refused to move as the ogre stepped out of the cover of the trees and closed on him. "You don't have a chance of taking me anywhere. You know that, right?"

The ogre towered over him. Shaggy hair hung over his eyes. His clothes were made of burlap and leather with a thick, wide, black belt around his waist. A long sheath hung low on his right hip. He growled deep in his throat as he moved to stand in front of Wayne. He laid his hand on the hilt of his sword, his thick fingers curling around the pommel. "I will force you to go if you choose to be stubborn."

"If all you're doing is delivering a message, why do you need to be armed? I can't be all that dangerous to you."

"I never go anywhere without my sword. It's a great persuader." The ogre leaned close to Wayne's face. "And I may use it if you become difficult."

"Aw, you guessed my plan. We mortals can be very contradictory when the situation demands it."

He forced himself to take a step back and change the tone of his voice. Maybe a little diplomacy would help. After all, it had gotten him out of some hard conversations with clients. He frowned at how deep his voice had gotten. What happened to him? He was now almost eye level with the ogre in front of him. "You can't intimidate me, and I'm trying to be respectful. I've had some experience with supernatural beings, and you don't strike me as threatening. Now, tell me how you found me. I've never contacted you or your tribe."

"We felt you when you opened the door to the Dark Lands." The ogre leaned closer to him. "We claim you as one of us. You are part of the ogre tribe, and you will rejoin with your village. Chief Argus has demanded your return. Your power will help defend us, and with your heritage, your power rightfully belongs to the tribe."

Wayne barked out a harsh laugh. "I don't believe this. You mean the same tribe who surrendered my father to the Huntsman? The same tribe responsible for my mother's death? And now he wants me only for what I can give him? Sorry, but that won't happen now or ever. We're done here."

The ogre made a strangling sound, which Wayne supposed could be a laugh. "Boy, your lineage has shown itself in your appearance."

"I don't know what you mean."

A buzzing started in his ears to add to the nausea

churning in his stomach. He rubbed his forehead, but it didn't feel right. Had he changed somehow? He lowered his hand and almost didn't recognize it. His hand could easily be twice its normal size, and his fingers had swelled to the size of sausages. He had changed and had no idea how it happened. Could this shapeshift be responsible for the sudden onset of nausea?

"What did you do to me? Did you cast a bizarre spell with some freaky ogre magic or something?"

"I did not change you in any way. Tell me why you mock me with how you shapeshift."

The ogre stepped closer, and Wayne felt his body shift even more.

"Your true heritage has come out, boy. You will return with me now."

"I don't think so." Wayne turned his back on the ogre to repack his bag. "Your chief can demand my presence all he wants, but he doesn't have any claim on me. I have no family with the ogres. Not after what they did to my parents. Go tell your chief I'll never come to the Dark Lands or the ogre tribe."

"I'll deliver your disrespectful message. Trust me when I say you will have no choice but to return."

"There's always a choice." Wayne snatched up his purchases. "Feel free to tell your chief what I said."

As he walked away, he sensed the ogre's glare stab him between his shoulder blades. He had no love for a tribe responsible for the destruction of his family. The more the distance opened up between him and the monstrous messenger, the faster the nausea went away. By the time he reached the edge of the park, his stomach settled like he'd never felt ill at all. He held his hand up, and it appeared as it usually did.

A small woman fell into step beside him. He gave her a glance before he turned to stare straight ahead. She stood about four feet tall with fair skin and brown hair and freckles across the bridge of her nose. She could be called portly, with her round belly and double chin.

"Do I know you?"

She flashed him a quick smile as her eyes sparkled with mirth.

"Look, I don't know if you're laughing at me, but I'm not very good company right now. I've got a lot on my mind. If you're lost, the town hall is right there." He frowned when she walked next to him as he headed back to Main Street. "I don't want to be rude, so you should probably go."

The little woman chuckled as she kept up with him. "No, Master Wayne. I'm not lost, nor am I laughing at you. I'm laughing at the way you put that ogre in his place. I saw and heard the whole thing from the safety of the trees. I'm here to guide you. My name is Hildegard. I'm a gnome, and I've been sent to help you."

He stopped short, and she walked a few paces, then turned.

"I really don't need a guide. How did you even find me? First an ogre says I have a tribe to return to, and now you show up out of the blue." He sighed as his shoulders slumped before he finally smiled. "This is turning out to be a heck of a day. Are you sure you don't want to go home? I promise I don't need any help."

She fell into step beside him as he continued down the street. "I understand you haven't had the best morning, but I am here to help. My master has sent me with specific instructions to guide and protect you to the best of my abilities."

"Oh yeah? Who is this mysterious master who wants me protected?"

"The Ferryman." She stopped when he did. "The Ferryman is my employer, and I do what he tells me to."

"You know, before I came to Garland Falls, I would've thought you were crazy. Now I'm no longer surprised at anything people tell me." He stared at her in her modern button-down shirt, sneakers, and blue jeans. Long blonde braids hung down each side of her face. "I'm not sure how you can protect me. You don't even carry a weapon."

"There are more ways to protect someone than with weapons, Master Wayne."

"Aren't you supposed to wear peasant clothes and a pointy hat?"

She laughed out loud and held her stomach. "Heavens no, Master Wayne. We haven't dressed in those fashions since the 1700s. I have more skills in defense than you would believe. I am capable of keeping you from harm." She pointed to the sky. "The rainbow led me to you. Leprechauns and rainbows go together like ice cream and chocolate sauce."

He stooped down and laid his hands on her shoulders. "You can see it?" He hung his head and smiled when she nodded. "I'm glad someone else here can, and I love the analogy. Well, is there somewhere you can go? I have a lunch date soon, and I wouldn't want you to…"

"Cause a distraction?" Hildegard chuckled and bowed. "I can see the rainbow because leprechauns, gnomes, brownies, and all the rest like us are connected. We all share almost the same type of magic." She patted his hand. "I shall meet you at Delia Warner's establishment tonight. She and I have been friends for a long time."

When she walked away, Wayne shook his head. The amount of people who knew Miss Dee no longer surprised him. He would have been more surprised if she didn't know Miss Dee. He leaned against a storefront and rubbed his head. He'd come to Garland Falls for a party and after a skeleton woman in his dreams told him to. Life in New Jersey was good, but he'd never had anything so interesting happen to him until he'd come to Garland Falls.

His thoughts turned to the ogre who had confronted him in the park. How had he known where Wayne was at that point in time? Would the ogres find him again or make him go to the Dark Lands? Why did his leprechaun luck always decide to turn bad right when he needed it to be good? His bad personal luck had to be the catalyst that had drawn the ogre to him. It just figured.

However, he now had Eleanor in his life. She'd become the one bright spot, and he found himself wanting to be with her more and more. At the party, they'd danced most of the night away. Smart, beautiful, fun, and she liked him more than anyone else there. He let her fill his mind, and a slight breeze blew his hair into his eyes. He pushed his hair back and noticed a storefront across the street. A "for rent" sign appeared in the window where he knew there hadn't been one a few minutes ago. He rolled his eyes. Garland Falls did want to try to make him stay.

"We'll see, my little town. We'll see."

A pickup truck pulled to a stop in front of him, and Lucas Callahan leaned over the seat as he rolled down the window. "Hey, Wayne. Are you lost? Which would be strange because you're on Main Street in the middle of town."

Wayne walked over and leaned on the door. "Hi, Lucas. No, I'm not lost. I have a lot on my mind right now." He forced out a smile as he gazed into the truck. "You're out and about early today."

"I have to pick up some supplies from the hardware store. For some reason, most of the plant stakes I bought a couple of weeks ago broke in record time."

"Can I help? I'm more of an office person, but you helped me with the invitation and the key to the Dark Lands. I'd like to repay the favor."

"Sure. Hop in." Lucas started the truck after Wayne settled himself in the passenger seat. "My assistant is out on his honeymoon right now. When he gets back, he wants to put his house up for sale."

"His new wife must have a pretty great home if he wants to sell his place."

Lucas parked in front of Lou's Hardware and shut the engine off. "She owns a big manor house right down the street from his old house. I guess no one wants to own two houses, right? Double the property, double the expense."

"I've always thought so. Speaking as an accountant, it's not good financial sense either. I'll wait for you here."

He didn't believe a store and a house coming up empty at the same time could be a coincidence. Could his being here be so important to the town and everyone? What would it mean for what he'd built for himself back east? He'd worked hard to get the partnership. He watched people walk past the truck and smiled at their conversations and quiet laughter. In Garland Falls, he didn't have to always be the perfect business man. He rolled his shoulders, finally noticing most of the tension had eased.

He sighed and knew this was what people meant by being torn in two. He wanted to go back. He wanted to stay in this town. Of course, more and more incidents made it harder for him to want to go back. The biggest one could be the electric zoom in his veins for Eleanor Keyes. If he remained here, she would be the biggest reason for his decision. Of course, he now had more friends here besides Renee. He also liked being able to feel his shoulders relax. He laid his head back and closed his eyes. Maybe he'd let the thoughts and indecision tumble through his mind to sort themselves out. As one of his favorite songs said, only time would tell.

Chapter Eight

Wayne pulled off the thick work gloves before he wiped his forehead. For early March, the sun shone hotter and brighter than he'd thought it would. He glanced at the sky, and the rainbow still hovered above him. He couldn't believe how much brighter the colors were after he worked with the plants and flowers. Definitely something to do with his leprechaun half.

"You know, I never considered myself to be the outdoor worker type, but this is a great way to relax." He looked at the rainbow again. "You still can't see the rainbow, can you?"

Lucas glanced at the sky and shook his head. "No, no rainbow up there for me to see. Those are more with your lineage." He pushed his black cowboy hat back and hung his gloves in his waistband. "And I have to agree with you about working with flowers. There's a peace in nature you can't find anywhere else. As a Green Man, it's part of my job to be in the outdoors. To give joy to someone else with flowers makes it all worthwhile."

"Is there any other job we need to do right now?" When Lucas shook his head, Wayne checked the time. "It's almost one, and I have a lunch date. Can you give me a lift back to Main Street?"

"Sure." Lucas led the way to the greenhouse and put their gloves on the worktable. He yanked his car keys out of his pocket as they walked to his truck. "I can use a bite to eat myself."

On the short drive back, Wayne glanced at his friend. "Can I tell you about some odd stuff?"

"Sure. How can I help?"

Wayne took a deep breath, unsure how to begin. "When I touch doors, they either turn purple or gold. Parker said the purple door leads to the Dark Lands. After what I saw there, I believe him. Where does the gold door lead?"

"The Light Side. Your heritage is in both lands, but they shouldn't open for you. Parker, myself, and the Keeper of the Keys are the only ones supposed to be able to open all the doors." He glanced at Wayne. "But we all need keys to do it. I'm not sure how they open at your touch."

"This is so strange. Doors turn colors and open for me when they shouldn't. A rainbow has started to follow me. I can see it, but no one else can. My pockets are always filled with leprechaun gold. Mac says I need to move here to help people with their bookkeeping and finances. A store comes up for rent when I looked at it. Now you tell me there's a house for sale here soon. What am I supposed to think?"

Lucas grinned. "How about you're supposed to give serious consideration to a move here? I know I could use some accounting help with my business. Unlike leprechauns, most of us don't have the skill to work with finances."

"And now you've jumped on the 'making me move' bandwagon." Wayne grinned. "Is there some sort of conspiracy to get me here?"

"Not that I'm aware of, but hey. I'm only a gardener." Lucas parked in front of the diner, and they waved to Eleanor. "How about this, then? There's a lady who I believe is infatuated with you."

Wayne smiled at Eleanor as they approached her. "We only met a few days ago, but I have talked to her more since then. How can you be so certain?"

"It's part of my power as a Green Man. I can always sense when love is in the air. I felt the same way when I met my wife, and I could see it in my brother. I also sensed it in my assistant when he met the woman he married." He clapped Wayne on the shoulder. "You've fallen for her as hard as she's fallen for you. Don't fight it. You guys will be great together."

Wayne hurried over to Eleanor. She looked prettier than she had that morning. He glanced at the sky, and the rainbow appeared to arc down over her head. She had to be the person he should have in his life. A rainbow wouldn't lie to a leprechaun, would it?

"We have good timing to get here at the same moment." Eleanor waved to Lucas before he walked off as Wayne took her hand. "Or is it good luck we seem to be together a lot?"

"I think I'll stay with the good luck. I could use some right now."

He escorted her in, and they headed to an empty booth.

As soon as they sat, a waitress with red hair and a ready smile hurried over to them. "Hi, Eleanor. I didn't think you'd ever bring a date in here to meet me."

"Hi, Sally. This is Wayne Billings. He's Renee Callahan's friend from back east."

"I came in for the party, and I wanted to use some of my vacation time, so I'm here for an extended visit."

"Nice to meet you, Wayne. I'll get your water while

you check out the menu. We've got some of your favorites on there, Eleanor."

As Sally scurried off, Wayne opened the menu. "All the food sounds so good, but I think the turkey sandwich sounds perfect."

Eleanor nodded. "I had the same thought myself. Of course, french fries are a must with any sandwich, or are you a potato chip kind of guy?"

"French fries all the way. I save the chips for cookouts and barbecues."

When Sally returned, they gave her their order and watched as she ran off again.

Wayne stared after her. "If she keeps up such a hectic pace, she'll wear herself out before she's forty."

"You'd be surprised at her true age."

He sat back and drummed his fingers on the table. "Let me guess. She's an elf and is hundreds of years old. Part of her power makes her look like she's in her thirties."

"It's simpler than what you said, but yes, she is in her thirties. She loves the hectic pace of this place. She says it keeps her young."

"She looks like she's in good shape."

Eleanor smacked the back of his hand. "Have you been checking out other women on our lunch date? I'm very surprised at you."

He turned his hand over and held hers. "Of course not. I'm sure Sally has dozens of men who pine after her on a daily basis."

"You're right, but no one's caught her eye yet."

Sally brought their sandwiches and scurried off again to greet more customers. They ate in silence, even though Wayne had dozens of questions he wanted to ask her. He finished, wiped his mouth, and sat back. He had no idea how to broach the subject he wanted answers to, so he decided to jump in with both feet.

"Do you believe in magic and fairies and all the rest that goes with it?" He kept his gaze focused on the table so he wouldn't see her reaction. "I never used to, but circumstances have changed recently."

"Of course I do. You can't live in Garland Falls and not believe." She tapped her fingers on the table as she studied him. "If you didn't believe before, what made you believe now?"

He looked up when Sally returned and ordered them each a slice of key lime pie. "There's been some odd occurrences, which happened to me on my first visit here. They even continued after I went back home."

"Is this about your heritage?" She sat back and moved her silverware around. "Your lineage might have tuned you in to the unseen worlds."

His head jerked up. "You know about me?"

"Renee told me." She smiled her thanks when Sally set their dessert down. "I have my own unique origins also. As a matter of fact, there aren't many people in Garland Falls who don't have some magic or fairy blood in them." She leaned across the table. "They say you have to have some magic in you to find Garland Falls."

"I'm not surprised, but if that were true, how do the tourists get here?"

She sat back and picked up her fork. "The town likes all the people, and the elders theorized Garland Falls likes its people to be prosperous."

"Makes sense." He picked at the pale-green pie slice in front of him. "I'm supposed to go back home after St. Patrick's Day. However, everyone I talk to tries to convince me to move here. Garland Falls itself also put the thought in my head."

She smiled at him as she nibbled her pie. "Would a move here be so bad? It's clear the people and the town like you very much."

"Did you say the town likes me?" He rolled his eyes when she nodded. "After what you've told me, I shouldn't be surprised. Not sure why I am. Tell me about the town."

"Garland Falls is hard to describe."

They finished their lunch, and Wayne paid the bill before they walked back to her store.

"The families who founded Garland Falls built the town on a nexus point so fairies, pixies, and everyone else could go home when they wanted. There are some regular humans here, and most of the tourists who come are mortal." She stored her purse in her office and turned. "There are others, like you and me, who have a more supernatural lineage."

He leaned on the counter. "I had a sense you were like me. I'm half ogre and half leprechaun. Who are your parents?"

She smiled as she took down the "back at two" sign. "You aren't ready to learn about me yet. There are situations I've been told you need to experience for yourself first."

"Again, I'm not surprised to *not* get a straight answer. Garland Falls has a lot of questions I need answers to, and yet it never wants to share."

She laughed. "Very true, but the town and the people know information must be found out in order. If not, chaos would reign over all of us."

"I guess you're right. We wouldn't want chaos

running rampant." He noticed chairs with a small table in a quiet corner. "Do you mind if I sit and read for a little while? The atmosphere is so calm in here, and I think I need some quiet right now."

"Of course not. You stay here as long as you like." She walked him over to the area. "If you want some tea or water a little later, I can get it for you."

"Thanks. I'll let you know."

He opened the book he'd bought about ogres and began to read. The more he tried to concentrate on the ogre history, the more his mind wandered. Before long, the words swam before his eyes and he dozed off. Someone shook his shoulder and called his name. He forced his eyes to open, blinking several times to clear his vision. He looked up at Eleanor, and she smiled at him.

"Wake up, Wayne. It's time for me to close for the day."

He stared at his watch. He'd been asleep for several hours. "I'm sorry. I must have been more tired than I thought. I'd better get back to the B and B. Will I see you tomorrow?"

She pulled him to his feet and held his hands. "You can come see me as often as you like."

"If I could, I don't think I'd ever leave here." He glanced around the store, the quiet music, the books with their smell of ink and probably a little dust. "You make everything in here feel special."

"Thank you. I'd love for you to be here with me all the time, but we'll have to see what the future holds." She stepped closer and laid her hand on his cheek. "Please think about moving here. I don't care what anyone else says. I'd love for you to be here all the time."

"I'm starting to feel the same way."

He didn't want to let go of her hands and drive back to the B and B. The more he stayed around her, the more he never wanted to leave her side. He helped her clean the store and organize a few books to be shelved. They worked together in companionable silence until he could delay his departure no longer.

He laid his hand on hers and squeezed her fingers. "Thanks for letting me help you."

She wrapped her arms around his waist in a tight hug. "Thanks for staying to help."

He walked out to his car and watched as she turned out the lights. He drove back to the B and B and missed her smile and warmth already. For a short drive, the loneliness hit him in the stomach like a prize fighter. He forced down what he suspected could be tears as he pulled into the parking lot.

"I'm back, Miss Dee."

She came out of the kitchen with a sandwich on a plate and some fruit off to the side. "A heavy meal won't let you sleep. Try this, and I saved you a cinnamon roll for dessert. I sensed you might be a tad upset this evening and needed some comfort food."

He gave her a quick hug and grinned. "You're an absolute wonder, Miss Dee. Thank you for this."

"Oh, pish tosh. I love to take care of my customers. Now eat up and get some rest."

He listened to Dee bustle around in the kitchen while he ate. The light dinner sat comfortably in his stomach as he stood and stretched. His eyelids drooped, and he dragged himself up the stairs to his room. Right now, sleep would be better than any dessert except the cinnamon rolls.

"Good evening, Master Wayne. I trust you had a pleasant afternoon?"

He yawned, too tired to care how Hildegard had appeared out of nowhere in his room. "Yes, I had a nice afternoon. Eleanor and I had a wonderful time. Did you keep yourself busy?"

"Yes. Delia and I had a wonderful chat. It's so nice to catch up on the latest scuttlebutt from time to time." She gestured to the bed. "I have laid out your bedtime garments. Should I help you undress?" She reached for the belt on his pants, and he jumped away.

"No, you don't have to help me undress. I can get myself changed." He laid a hand on her shoulder. "I'm sorry I wasn't in the best mood when we met. I promise I'll be better behaved from now on. Good night, Hildegard. See you tomorrow."

"No apologies needed, Master Wayne. I wish you sweet dreams and good rest. I shall come to you tomorrow in case you need my help."

When she disappeared, he climbed into bed and smiled. He loved the joy in Hildegard's personality. Not the kind of joy Eleanor gave him, but her sunny disposition eased some of the worries he'd felt ever since the ogre incident in the park. Questions still floated in his mind about how the ogre had found him in the first place. Why had nausea crawled through him? How had his features started to change?

For the ogre to demand Wayne return to the Dark Lands had to be the most ludicrous statement he'd ever heard. Like he'd ever go there on his own. Answers could wait until morning. Since Eleanor—and yes, she'd showed up in his thoughts again—had supernatural origins, she might know what to do. He stared at all the doors he'd opened before he got into bed. No surprises in the morning when he got up if he could help it.

He yawned and turned over. Tomorrow, he'd have to ask Hildegard if she knew why the ogre chief wanted him back. The ogres had ousted his father from the tribe, so why come after him? He didn't understand how he could be important now. If it had something to do with the rainbow or the gold coins, he'd be surprised. Those were apparently tied to the leprechauns, not the ogres.

Chapter Nine

Wayne tossed and turned all night. Dreams plagued him with ogres on one side and leprechauns on the other. They fought over who would get to keep him. He protested, and both sides grabbed his arms and pulled until he thought they'd rip his arms off. He thrashed around before he fell out of bed, his legs wrapped like a mummy in the sheet.

He massaged his temples to try and ease the massive headache throbbing behind his eyes. Right now, if he could believe the dream, both sides wanted him. He moved his head from side to side as he tried to loosen his neck muscles. Well, he wanted no part of either side. Unfortunately, he needed to contact both tribes to find out about his powers and what he could do.

When he opened the bathroom door, once again the Dark Lands stretched out before him. He slammed the door shut, and when he opened it again, the Light Side lands appeared. His jaw clenched as he tried one more time, and it opened into the bathroom attached to his room. This constant worry about which land he would see behind the closed doors had started to wear him out.

He frowned. He'd opened all the doors before he went to bed. How come they were all shut now? If he'd started sleep walking, he'd officially throw in the metaphorical towel.

A soft knock pulled his attention to the door, and he

opened the it. Hildegard stood there, his robe draped over one arm, and she smiled. He stepped to the side and let her in. She held his robe out, and he slipped into it.

"Thank you, Hildegard." He gestured around the room. "Did you close all the doors in here?"

"Yes, Master Wayne. I feared imps had gotten into your room and played a trick." She wrung her hands, and tears filled her eyes. "I'm sorry if I erred. Did you mean to have them open?"

"Yes. I opened them and left them like that, but it's okay. You didn't know." He perched on the bed and smiled at her. He took her hands in his. "No imps, no tricks. I had a few bad dreams is all. Can you step outside for a minute so I can get dressed?"

"Of course, Master Wayne." She patted his knee. "If you have need of me, call out. I'll be right outside."

His shoulders sagged, and he hung his head. "I'll let you know when I'm ready. I have a couple of questions to ask you."

She handed him his shirt. "Of course. I will tell you all I can."

When she left, his mind filled with indecision. He should leave here, but he couldn't. The thought of leaving soured his stomach and hurt his heart. If he left, he wouldn't see Eleanor anymore. He'd promised Renee he'd stay until after St. Patrick's Day. And with how this town celebrated holidays, St. Patrick's Day would have some great events planned.

At the thought of Eleanor, his heart thumped in his chest. Fluttery tickles in his stomach made him grin. Lucas was right. He had a serious infatuation with the lovely book lady. They hadn't even known each other a week yet. He crossed his fingers and hoped his bad personal luck would behave itself. She seemed to be made for him. Of course, he could say he was made for her, too.

He called Hildegard back into the room and let her sit on the bed. "The other day, you know the day we met, an ogre came out of the woods and demanded I return to the tribe."

The gnome frowned. "I know he shouldn't have been able to leave the Dark Lands. What he said concerns me."

"The ogre chief wants me back. We both heard him say that. My question is why? Why come after me all these years later and want whatever power the chief claims I possess? I think it's important I know as much as possible in case any more ogres show up."

Hildegard hopped off the bed and walked to the window. She stood silently as she gazed over the yard. When she still refused to answer, Wayne came up behind her and laid his hand on her shoulder.

"Hildegard, do you know what my power is and why the ogres think it's so important?"

She turned to him and put her hand over his. "With your ogre and leprechaun heritage, you should be able to combine what you can do into a powerful magic source. The chief wants to make sure you don't use this ability against him. He never should have banished your father and made his family outcasts after their fight. You'd still live in the village if he hadn't."

Wayne closed his eyes and shook his head. His breath constricted in his chest, and he wiped his clammy hands on his pants. "So for the sake of one fight, the chief sold my father and me out to the Huntsman."

"It would appear so." She pulled the curtains aside

and pointed to the sky. "Look to the rainbow, Master Wayne. Its light will guide and protect you when you need it most. It has always been a beacon of hope and strength to the leprechaun clans."

He held out three coins. "And what about the gold coins that show up in my pockets every day? Parker Callahan told me these are leprechaun gold."

"That they are." She curled his fingers around them and patted his hands. "They may be able to help you more than you realize."

He plopped down on the window seat, the sun warming his back. He opened and closed his mouth several times before he could get any words out. "Thank you, but can you give me some time alone? I need to process this."

"Of course, Master Wayne. I understand there's a lot you need to consider."

****

Sunlight shone through the window, and Eleanor groaned. She'd gotten very little rest as her thoughts turned over and over in her mind. She always had gotten better rest at her father's home. Her flesh-and-blood form needed to sleep, not just lay down and rest. She'd wanted to return to the Dark Lands, but a deep ache made her bones creak and groan. Well, she could take a hint and stayed in her apartment.

As she made her breakfast, her thoughts returned to Wayne. She hoped she'd see him today. She enjoyed his company a little too much. She loved every time he helped her out in the store. For a highly paid and important accountant, cleaning and stocking a small bookstore should have been beneath him. His smile told her he liked helping out with the mundane tasks she accomplished every day.

She held her hand up and curled her fingers into a fist and then straightened them out. Hard to believe the flesh, muscle, blood, and veins were hers here in the mortal world. She could feel her bones hidden by the fragile skin as they moved. In the Dark Lands, she was nothing but bone. She'd never been conflicted about her dual identity before. What had changed her perspective about herself?

"I don't know which form makes me happy anymore." She looked at her hands and sighed. "Am I flesh and blood, or am I dry bones?"

All of this uncertainty had started when she first dreamed of Wayne, and the indecision annoyed her to no end. She sighed and rested her chin on her hand. If he'd been a normal human, she could have passed off this infatuation without any problems. But his heritage proclaimed him to be from the fairy realms. Not one realm either. He had to be both Dark Lander and Light Sider.

"Good morning, Mistress Eleanor."

She smiled when Hildegard walked into the kitchen. "Hi, Hildegard. I thought Dad said you were to stay with Wayne and guide him."

"Master Wayne asked me some difficult questions when he woke. His power has confused him more and more. Now the ogres want to possess it. Your premonition must be right. The time will come when the leprechauns also try to stake their claim. He asked if he could have some time to himself." The gnome took a small pastry. "I thought I would come to see how you fared today."

"I didn't rest very well last night." Eleanor rose and

went to the sink to wash her few dishes. "It's strange, but I know Wayne could be in serious trouble and soon. I wish I knew who and when."

"Master Wayne has already had interaction with a member of the ogre tribe." She finished her pastry and wiped her mouth. "You could have sensed the leprechauns. Don't worry, mistress. All will become clear to you when the time is right."

She stooped down to hug the gnome. "You sound like Mom. Thank you, Hildegard. I don't know what I'd do without you."

Eleanor hurried to get ready and head to her shop on time. Her heart beat faster at the thought she'd see Wayne. She hoped he'd come to the bookstore again. She smiled when she remembered how he looked as he slept in the chair at the back of the store. His brow had smoothed out, and he'd looked even more handsome.

His light-brown hair hung over his eyes, and he didn't appear quite so polished. He reminded her of a little boy who'd conquered the monster under his bed. Several times, she'd been tempted to wake him, but he'd looked like he needed the rest. What dreams kept him up at night? She knew it couldn't be her, so who wanted him so much? She made a mental note to ask him about it today if she had the time.

She got the store ready and flipped the sign to open. With her store across the street from Renee's, she could watch for Wayne easier from her front counter. She had no doubt he'd stop in. She laid a hand over the heart she possessed here in the mortal world. He must feel the same pull between them. Otherwise, she fabricated the whole relationship in her mind. She'd never been so fanciful over a man before, so what made him so different? Wayne made her bones thrum with sensations she'd never felt in her bony life. Her mother would say it's love since love was stronger than mere infatuation.

She walked back to the storeroom and stared at the door. It had a different vibe than yesterday morning. Wayne had stared at this door when she found him. She reached her hand out and paused. She took a deep breath as she grabbed the knob and yanked the door open. Inside sat her overstock and the usual supplies. The contents hadn't changed, so why had Wayne looked spooked when she found him there?

She grabbed several titles she needed and headed back to the front of the store. The Irish book display needed to be refreshed. She moved some books around, added the ones she'd brought out, and wiped the table down. The bell chimed, and she turned to greet her first customers of the day.

As the lunch hour approached, she wondered where Wayne could be. Hadn't he said he would be by today? Despite the chill in the air, a lot of tourists strolled down Main Street. She'd had good sales before lunch, but her hands shook as she waited for Wayne to show up.

She opened the door and stepped outside. She shielded her eyes as she looked at the sky. Wait. How could a rainbow be present now? The colors shone bright against the wispy clouds and the cerulean blue of the sky. The conditions weren't right for one, but there it shone, bright as the sun. Hildegard had told her Wayne always saw a rainbow. It must be tied to him, which meant he had to be nearby.

****

"Hey, Renee." Wayne walked in and unbuttoned his coat. "Why is it so warm in here?"

"I don't know. I shut the heat off, but I think the system has gone a little wonky. I hired someone to come by this afternoon to take a look at it. What can I help you with today?"

He ran his fingers along the one case and kept his focus on the items on display. "I thought I'd say hi. We need to schedule a time for us to get together before I leave." He walked over to stare at the bags on the wall. "I thought I'd ask Eleanor to come too if you wouldn't mind."

She hurried around her workstation and grabbed him in a hug. "Of course, it's okay. Eleanor is a good friend, and so are you. I'm glad the two of you have hit it off. I told you your luck would turn around and you'd meet someone."

"I know how quick a romantic situation can go south for me, though. It's happened before. But what about the skeleton woman from my dream? She hasn't contacted me again. She said it's dangerous to do dream speak." He glanced out the window to the bookstore across the street. "She reminds me of Eleanor. I'm not sure how or why. Maybe it's the way she speaks."

Renee also stared at the store across the street. "I've never seen her turn into a skeleton, but everyone in this town has some kind of a secret. I'm glad they aren't the spooky or creepy kinds of secrets. Though I guess you could call a skeleton spooky."

"I guess so." He smiled at her and nudged her shoulder. "At least a skeleton is the only spooky secret. But the skeleton woman from my dream, she's different. I'm not afraid of her, and she doesn't strike me as the spooky type." He refocused his gaze on the other store. "There's something else I want to tell you. Almost every time I touch a door, it opens into a different land. Lucas says you need a key to open those. Then he said he, Parker, and someone called the Keeper of the Keys are the only ones who have access. No one else does, so how can I open these doors?"

"I have to admit you have some strange stuff in your life right now. I'm sure your magic is the reason behind it all. Have you talked to Miss Dee or Mrs. Hall about this?"

He shook his head. "No. It took me forever to get up the nerve to ask Lucas about it, though. Do you think I need to see this Keeper of the Keys person?"

"Wouldn't do you any good right now. She's out of town on her honeymoon."

"Quite a coincidence because Lucas said his assistant took time off for his honeymoon." A small frown creased his brow. "Does everyone get married at the same time around here?"

She nudged his shoulder back with her own. "Of course not. Who do you think Lucas' assistant married? He wants to sell his house on Darkling Street so he can move in with his new wife. You should check it out. It might be the right enticement to make you move here."

"Not you, too." Wayne laid his head back and groaned. "Almost everyone I talk to, including Garland Falls itself, wants me to move here."

"Because we all sense you belong here. You'd be a fantastic addition to the town." She led him to her back room, and they sat. "Wayne, you have magic in you. When you came here, it woke up. Garland Falls knows you need to be with your own kind."

He sat back and stared at her. "Yes, but which kind? I have ogres after me. I dream about leprechauns saying

I belong with them. The town talks to me. If Garland Falls wants me here, it needs to be clearer with its intentions." A loud groan reached him, and he sat straight up. "What the heck was that?"

"The town." She folded her arms, and a smug smile crossed her face. "Trust me. This town is very special, and we don't have an actual accountant yet. I'm sure you'd have more clients than you could count if you made Garland Falls your home."

"How do I get the town to not want to send me to the Dark Lands or the Light Side?"

She took his hands. "There may be a reason why the doors open for you. Garland Falls always has a reason for what it does. Your double heritage could be why. I hope it isn't someone on the other side trying to entice you over."

"I can agree with you wholeheartedly on that statement."

He stood, and she followed.

"I wish the town would tell me this particular reason. It's hard to get dressed if my clothes aren't there." He checked the time on his phone. "I have to go. I want to take Eleanor to lunch again. I got out of Miss Dee's later than I expected. I told her I'd be by, and I don't want her to think I forgot."

"Tell her I said hi."

Wayne left as Renee got back to work and customers filed in. He hurried across the street and stepped into the bookstore. He didn't see Eleanor at the counter, so he headed for the closest aisle. Halfway down he heard her voice on the other side of the shelves. He walked around the corner and stopped.

She laughed with a tall, handsome gentleman who

smiled at her. His pale skin looked almost white, and his clothes hung loose on his bone-thin frame. Wayne took a deep breath and tried not to stare at the man as he made his way over to them. Did his personal luck turn bad already? It always did when he found someone he liked.

"Hi, Eleanor. Sorry I'm so late. I didn't sleep well, and I went to see Renee for a little bit."

"It doesn't matter. You're here now." She took his hand and tugged him closer. "I'm glad you made it. Wayne, this is my father. Dad, this is Wayne Billings."

Wayne shook his hand. "It's nice to meet you, Mr. Keyes."

"Same here. Eleanor talks about you all the time." He smiled as he laid his arm across Eleanor's shoulders. "It's nice to have a face to go with the name. Well, I won't keep you. I know it's almost time for your lunch break." He kissed her forehead. "I'll see you tonight."

After her father left, Wayne turned to her. "Does he feel all right? I've never seen anyone so thin and so pale."

"Dad has had a thin body and pale complexion most of his life. He's in fine health, I mean for how bad he looks."

She hung her "back at two" sign on the door, and they headed to the diner again.

"I'm so glad you got to meet him."

"Me, too." He took meeting her father as a sign of good luck. "Let's hurry before the diner fills up."

They ordered sandwiches as the crowd pushed in behind them, so they ate quickly. As soon as they left, a couple took their booth. Wayne checked out the packed diner while he paid. Sal's always had a huge crowd no matter what time of day he got there. They meandered down to her store arm in arm.

Eleanor squeezed his arm. "I enjoy having extra time with you."

"Renee wants us to get together for dinner one night." He laced his fingers through hers. "I'd like you to come with me."

"I thought you'd never ask." She held his hand tighter. "I want to spend more time with you, too."

He gestured to Main Street. "There isn't a whole lot to do in Garland Falls. What do you have in mind?"

She nodded toward the park. "The St. Patrick's Day festival should kick off this weekend. There will be plenty to do then. Mrs. Hall made sure everyone had their booths up in time. I could use your help with my own booth. The booth is put together, but I need to haul the rest of my stock down there."

When he draped his arm around her shoulders, his heart filled with joy when she sighed and snuggled closer. "What happens if it rains?"

"It won't. Lucas and Parker talked to the nature fairies to make sure we have clear skies for the festival."

"I guess it helps to have connections. I don't think I'll ever get used to how I've started to accept fairies and the rest of the magic stuff." He sighed and pulled her tighter to his side. "I've started to get used to the town, too."

The mention of St. Patrick's Day sent a shiver up his spine, but from fear or anticipation? He'd bet on anticipation. He had no reason at all to feel uneasy. What did Garland Falls want to tell him now? Could more trouble be on the horizon? He hoped not. This small town in the middle of nowhere Minnesota had started to become way too complicated. He had to smile.

Somehow, going back his semi-normal, almost mundane life back east didn't hold much appeal anymore.

"I'd love to help you take stock down there." He glanced around at the decorations in store windows and green-and-white carnation flower baskets hanging from the light poles. "If Mrs. Hall is in charge, you know it will be a grand affair."

She squeezed his hand. "Mrs. Hall always goes all in. Would you like to come to my house for dinner tonight? I know Miss Dee makes better food, but we need a place to have a quiet conversation."

Wayne didn't have to think twice. "I'd love to come and see what you can do. I'm sure your food's as good as Miss Dee's. Tell you what. I'll even grab dessert."

She unlocked the door to her store. "Sounds great. Come get me at five when the store closes."

"See you then."

Another date with his beautiful Eleanor. He smiled. He liked to think of her as his. Warmth rushed through his veins the more he thought about her. He'd be honored if she felt the same. Ms. Eleanor Keyes had to truly be the one for him. Even the rainbow shone brightly over her store. He took it as a sign his luck had turned a corner.

Chapter Ten

Wayne stopped into Heavenly Bites and studied the selection in the case. He smiled as he listened to baby Marcus' wail echo from the back room. His dad always said being a parent had to be the hardest but most rewarding job a person could have. Davin's weary voice pleaded with the baby to stop his loud cries, and Wayne grinned even wider.

He straightened up when the new father came out of the back room. "Hi, Davin. I take it the baby isn't too happy right now?"

"Nope. I'll be glad when Joanna gets back. She had to run to Miss Dee's, and Marcus started up as soon as she left, and he hasn't stopped yet."

"I need to pick up some cookies for tonight. Should I come back later?"

"No, I got it." He held the baby out. "If you can hold on to this little guy for a few minutes, I can get you what you need."

Wayne held his arms out. "Sure, I guess. I've helped my friends with their babies. I think I remember how this works. Come here, little guy."

He took the baby, and Davin walked behind the counter. He bounced Marcus up and down while he picked out a large variety, not sure what Eleanor would like. The baby's cries slowed, then stopped when he grabbed Wayne's hair.

"Looks like you have the baby knack, Wayne." Davin boxed up his order and placed it on the counter. "You want to let me in on your secret?"

"I think you're too worried about when you hold him." He smiled at the baby who giggled and tugged on his hair harder. "You have to try and stay calm. Babies know when you're nervous. He's your first, isn't he?"

"How could you tell?"

They walked over to one of the tables, and Davin sank onto a chair.

"Jo's a natural, and so are you, but I can't find the best way to get comfortable with him."

Wayne pried the baby's fingers out of his hair and handed Marcus back to his father. "Every person has good parenting instincts. Trust yourself. You know what to do." He tapped Davin's chest over his heart. "They're right in there."

Marcus yawned and laid his head on Davin's shoulder. He rubbed the baby's back and murmured to him while Wayne watched. "Thanks, Wayne. You wouldn't consider a move here to babysit, would you?"

"And you're another one who wants me to move to Garland Falls. Davin, I'm an accountant, not a babysitter. Though this little guy is adorable." He stood and paced. "The more people tell me I need to move here, the more I'm considering it. Do you know why it's so important I live in Garland Falls?"

"Well, for one reason, this town needs a good accountant. I know I do. Hang on a second while I lay Marcus in his playpen." Davin disappeared for a few minutes, then returned without his son. "You see, the town wants new people here. The more we increase the population, the stronger the town becomes."

"And the town needs to be stronger, why?"

Davin smiled as he walked over to the box on the counter. "Sometimes, like the Halloween you came here, bad creatures or fairies try to come and wreak a little havoc. If the town is strong enough, we have a better chance to stop them before too much damage is done."

"I think I understand." He took the box from Davin and stared at it. "I don't know why Garland Falls has decided it needs me all of a sudden. I mean, I haven't been here since Renee's wedding a year ago."

Davin shrugged. "There could be a situation about to happen here or with you. If it's you, the town can give you a measure of security you can't find back east."

"So I've been told on numerous occasions." He lifted the box and grinned. "I guess we'll all find out when the time comes. Thanks, Davin."

He stepped outside and took a deep breath of the cool air. Renee had been right all those months ago. The air did smell better out here. He started toward Eleanor's store. Did he want to consider a move here? Leprechaun window stickers appeared to watch him as he passed. Goose bumps broke out on his arms, and he shivered. He checked over his shoulder more and more as he increased his pace. Sweat broke out on his forehead as he closed the distance to the bookstore.

His dream came back to him in detail. Ogres and leprechauns had fought over him and pulled at him until he thought he'd scream. Shadows kept pace with him as he hurried down the street. The night had never bothered him before, and he swallowed hard. Why should it bother him now and here of all places? He'd been told on numerous occasions he'd be safe here. A small person detached itself from the shadows, and he bit back a scream.

"Hildegard, you scared the life out of me." He clutched his chest and took deep breaths and prayed his heart stayed in its rightful place. "Why did you follow me?"

"I want to protect you." She took his hand and slowed his pace. "Please try to calm down. I sensed your distress and hurried to reach you. You never have to worry about anyone with malicious intentions as long as I'm around."

"Thanks." He took several deep breaths and could feel his blood pressure drop down to normal. He scanned the shadows and didn't trust what might be hiding there. "You didn't see anyone here, did you? You know, someone who wanted to follow me?"

"No, Master Wayne." Her eyes narrowed as she searched the area. "If anyone is here, they will have me to contend with. I promise you."

"Let's get to Eleanor's store. I don't know about you, but I'll feel better once we're inside."

"I agree with you." She lifted her head and sniffed several times. "There's mischief in the air tonight. Best to not linger out of doors."

They hurried down the street, and Wayne's shoulders sagged when he closed the door behind them. Eleanor stood at the counter as she rang up the last few customers of the day. Wayne waved and moved to scan the shelves while he waited for her to close up.

Eleanor walked back and smiled at them. "Hildegard, I didn't know you would be with Wayne."

"Master Wayne felt sure danger lurked around every corner." The gnome stood as tall as she could. "I have been charged with his protection. I came to keep him safe."

Eleanor hugged her. "You're the best, my friend. You can go home now. I'll take over the protection duty." She leaned close to whisper in a voice not too quiet. "We have a date tonight."

Hildegard grinned and bowed. "As you wish, ma'am. Have a nice time, you two."

Wayne watched as she produced a key and opened a door to step through. "I'm glad to find out how she comes and goes without no one the wiser. I thought only the Callahan boys and the Keeper person had keys, though."

"Sometimes, people on the other side can request passage. Let's get to my apartment and have some dinner. You didn't forget dessert, did you?"

He held up the bag from Heavenly Bites. "Got it right here. I'll follow you in my car, if you don't mind."

"How about if I ride with you? I don't drive often, and my apartment isn't too far away. I like to walk more than take my car."

He took her hands and smiled. "Leave it to the bookstore lady to have a better idea."

She didn't live far from her store. In less than ten minutes, they were at her apartment and inside. He sighed in relief to shut out the darkness as it descended over the town. He frowned. If sundown made his hands shake and goose bumps crawl up his spine, he couldn't wait to see how bad he'd get on the drive back to the B and B.

He inhaled, held it for a moment, then released it slowly and steadily. "I don't know what you made, but it smells great in here."

She walked into the kitchen and lifted the lid off a

pot on the stove. "I made stew and fresh bread."

He took his jacket off and hung it on the coatrack by the front door, then followed her into the kitchen. "Sounds amazing. I think it will go great with the cookies I got for dessert."

"I'm sure it will. Have a seat while I set the table and heat up dinner."

"Can I help you with any preparations?"

She turned and stumbled into his arms. He grabbed her around the waist to stop her before she fell over. They stared at each other for a few minutes before she smiled and laid her hands on his chest.

"No, it's easy stuff right now. I have everything handled."

"Then can I hold you a little longer?" He tightened his hands on her waist. When she gazed up at him, he knew exactly what he wanted to say. "You feel nice."

"You do, too."

They stood close to each other for another few minutes and didn't move and didn't say a word.

"If we don't break apart, we won't eat. I don't know about you, but I think I need some food."

"You're right." He smiled as he squeezed her one last time. "I knew you were smart."

He stepped away and watched her as she set the table and brought in the food. As she sliced the bread, he wondered when his bad luck would kick in. He considered this their third date. However, he hadn't made it to a fourth date in months. His leprechaun luck could be so unpredictable, and the uncertainty set his teeth on edge.

They sat at her dining room table, and she served him, then herself. "How much longer will you be in

Garland Falls?"

He buttered a piece of bread. "I'm booked at Miss Dee's until the day after St. Patrick's Day." As soon as he mentioned the holiday, the familiar uneasiness crawled through his body. "Of course, the way everyone talks to me, I'm supposed to move here."

"You have to do what makes you happy." She spooned a little more stew into her bowl. "Don't listen to anyone else. I mean, I know I said I'd love for you to move here, but that was selfish of me. You have to listen to your heart."

He picked up the slice of bread he buttered, then gazed at her. "My heart is telling me more and more I should be here. And I don't think you're selfish at all. Thank you for not dismissing how I feel."

"You're welcome. Eat up before it gets cold."

As they ate, she commanded his full attention. Her movements were graceful, and her smile full of light and laughter. Her blue eyes sparkled when she talked about books, her store, or her life in general. She liked his company and had invited him into her home. If Eleanor would be in his life, maybe a move to Garland Falls wouldn't be such a bad idea after all.

Chapter Eleven

After they ate, she led him to her living room and they sat on the couch. Wayne looked around, not surprised at how many bookshelves she owned. Pictures of nature scenes covered the walls, and the stereo sat in the corner with CDs and albums in their own shelves nearby. Several plants dotted the furniture, and all in all, it felt comfortable, homey, and lived in.

"You don't have a television?"

"No. There's no good shows on anyway, so why bother?"

He chuckled and put his arm around her shoulders and held her close. "You got me there. I have a television, but it's never on. Since I made partner at my firm, I don't have time to get involved in shows."

She gazed up at him. "You're a very busy man, aren't you? Maybe Garland Falls wouldn't be good for you after all. It's a slow-paced town. There aren't any big city activities to do here."

"I know, but I think that's the appeal of living here." He sat quietly for several minutes. "Eleanor, can I ask you a question?"

"Of course."

"Is there a chance you'd walk away from me?"

She sat up and stared at him. "Of course not. I like you very much, and I'm pretty sure you like me. Why do you ask?"

"Leprechaun luck isn't all it's cracked up to be. My business luck is phenomenal, but my personal life luck has bombed out more times than I can count. Tomorrow will be the fourth time we'll see each other. I've never made it past three with other women I've dated."

"We'll make it. You'll see." She settled back down next to him and smiled. "Maybe it's your ogre half. They aren't very big on love and dates and might put a crimp in your romance style. And we can count on our magic to help us through any rough spots that might creep up."

He chuckled and kissed the top of her head. "I guess you make a good point. I never gave it much thought. I certainly didn't take the magical element into consideration."

Eleanor sat up and glanced at the clock on the table. "Look at the time. It's late, and some of us have to work tomorrow. You will come back to the store, right?"

"You couldn't keep me away if you tried."

She walked him to the front door and looked up at him. "It's okay if you want to kiss me good night."

He leaned close, amazed by her crystal-blue eyes, which brought light to her heart-shaped face. He held her hands and stepped a little closer. He brushed her lips with a light kiss, and a whole different zing shot through him. She laid her hands on his cheeks and kissed him a little harder. Those crazy zings shot all through his body, and he feared he might catch fire. But what a way to go.

When he stepped back, he could see the surprised look in her eyes. Did surprise shine in his eyes, too? He suspected it did and would continue to do so. "Good night, Eleanor. I'll see you tomorrow."

"Good night, Wayne. I had a wonderful time with you."

He stepped outside, and all the good vibes faded as the darkness closed in around him. He zipped up his jacket and sprinted to his car. Once inside, he locked the doors while he searched for whatever phantom had spooked him. He started the drive to the B and B and told himself over and over he was safe. Maybe if he said it enough times, he'd believe it. Still, his gaze wouldn't stop flicking to the mirrors all the way to Miss Dee's.

He got to the B and B and rushed inside to lean against the door as his legs trembled with relief. The cheery atmosphere did its best to banish his unease, but tonight he found no comfort in the familiar rooms of Miss Dee's place. Time to get upstairs and lock the door. Maybe then he'd feel safe. He checked around, then sprinted up the steps.

"Hildegard? Are you here somewhere?"

No answer came back, and he missed the gnome. As matter of fact, he hadn't seen her since the afternoon. Eleanor must have told her they had a date and to take the night off. He'd wanted her advice about the strange uneasiness that coursed through his veins and tied his stomach into knots. He also wanted to talk to her about how he felt about Eleanor. He yawned. It could wait until the next day. He got ready for bed and slipped under the covers.

****

"Mistress Eleanor, wake up, wake up." Hildegard shook Eleanor hard. "I'm afraid Master Wayne has come to some harm."

"Hildegard?" Eleanor sat up and rubbed her eyes. "What do you mean? He was fine last night when he left. I know he went straight back to Miss Dee's. Tell me what's happened."

"He's gone, mistress." The gnome wrung her hands, and tears shone in her eyes. "I went to him this morning, like usual, and I couldn't find him."

"Did he have an early breakfast, or did he take a walk? I'm sure there's a simple explanation."

Hildegard shook her head hard. "No, no, no. Not an easy explanation here. His room was torn apart, and I found this." She held out a clump of black, coarse hair. "He's been taken to the Dark Lands. He isn't dressed to be there and doesn't have his invitation or his return key. They're in his jacket. Look." She held Wayne's jacket for Eleanor's inspection.

Eleanor examined the hair and scowled. "The ogres have him. I can't believe they'd be so bold to break into Miss Dee's place." She threw back the covers and stood. "Let's see if we can get him back. We'll stop at my dad's house and talk to him. He may have some advice for us."

The gnome waited while Eleanor dressed. The two sped to her store where she placed her "closed for personal emergency" sign in the window. She drove them up the hill to Warner's B and B. When they arrived, she walked the grounds to try to find Parker. She saw him as he worked around the gazebo and blew out a sigh of relief.

"Parker, I need your help."

He straightened up and turned. "Eleanor? What's wrong?" He glanced at Hildegard and nodded. "How can I help?"

"Wayne's been taken by ogres to the Dark Lands. Can you open the door?" She stared at the shed in the back corner. "I mean to get him back."

"Let's go." When they arrived, he put his hand on her arm. "Do you need a return key?"

"No. I can get back through my dad's house." She held up a jacket. "And we have Wayne's key." She smiled and kissed his cheek. "Thank you, Parker. Tell Renee I said hello and I can't wait for the four of us to have the dinner we talked about."

He put his hands together before he drew them apart. A large brass key formed between his hands. He knocked on the door three times, and the natural wood color changed to purple before he inserted the key.

"Be careful, Eleanor. Ogres aren't to be trusted."

She took a step to the open door. "I can trust a lot of the supernatural creatures there, and I know which ones to avoid. There's good and bad in the Dark Lands and the Light Side. Don't worry. Hildegard and I will be safe, and I'll return Wayne unharmed to Garland Falls."

"Let me know when you get back."

Eleanor took a deep breath and stepped through to her homeland, Hildegard right behind her.

****

Wayne rolled over and groaned. He didn't know what had happened but knew it couldn't be good. He remembered he'd gone to bed and he'd wanted to talk to Hildegard this morning. He'd slept most of the night before he heard a strange noise coming from his closet. He'd gotten up to investigate and didn't know what happened to him until he opened his eyes a moment ago.

"Well, isn't this terrific. At least my bad luck got me kidnapped and didn't sabotage my relationship with Eleanor." He groaned as aches and pains made themselves known, but he still chuckled. "I guess every bad situation does have some sort of silver lining."

He tried to move his arms and couldn't. He wiggled and squirmed and got himself to sit up, which made his head throb.

"Okay. I've been tied up by person or persons unknown." He closed his eyes and shook his head when he discovered he still wore the shorts and T-shirt he'd gone to bed in. "Great. Not only have I been taken in the middle of the night, but I'm not dressed for how cold it is here. This can't be good."

He struggled harder to get out of his bonds and winced when they pulled tighter. "Pajamas mean no jeans, shoes, decent shirt, or jacket." He leaned his head back. "And no jacket means no important invitation and no return key. That silver lining is starting to turn a little grayer."

He shrank back against the wall as the door banged open and weak sunlight flooded in. Now what? Like when the ogre confronted him in the park in Garland Falls, he refused to show fear. Whoever was coming in had better prepare themselves. He tugged on his bonds again. Yeah, be prepared to watch him wriggle like a fish out of water.

An older ogre woman walked in. Her stooped back and hunched shoulders brought her down to his height. The front of her dark-red skirt dragged on the ground while the back rode high above her ankles. A midnight-blue shirt hung outside the waistband of the skirt, and a colorful shawl covered her shoulders. Her black hair went to the top of her shoulders, and dark-brown leather boots covered her feet.

Her grin revealed uneven yellow teeth. "So the outcast son has returned to his tribe and is awake at last."

"If I hadn't been hit so hard, I would've been awake sooner." He shrugged and grinned at her. "Not complaining, just saying they could have been a little gentler when they grabbed me."

Well, she'd answered one question. He'd ended up in the ogre village, right where he never expected to be. He tried to be angry, but right now, he needed answers more than anything. The ogre chief had to have ordered him taken from Miss Dee's. The bonds around his legs were so tight the blood backed up, turning his skin bright red. He felt sure his arms looked the same from the swelling he could feel in his hands. He had no idea what would happen to him next, but it didn't look good for the home team.

"Look, I don't mean to be rude, but can you cut me loose? My hands and feet have gone numb, and every part of my body hurts."

She produced a small, wicked-looking knife from her skirt pocket. With a flick of her wrist, she had him free in seconds. "It's good to have you back where you belong."

"No. I belong in Garland Falls, with my friends. The ogres never wanted me before, so I'm not sure why they want me now." He rubbed his wrists to get feeling back into them. "And don't call me 'outcast.' My dad was an outcast, and now I'm a prisoner. This tribe has no right to keep me here, and I plan to leave as soon as I can." He stood and dusted himself off. He blinked several times before he supported himself against the wall. He must have been tied up longer than he realized. "Whoa. I didn't expect to be so light-headed. I need a minute."

"Come, boy." She took his arm and led him outside. "I can help with your aches and pains. The tonic I make will also help you straighten yourself out a bit."

Since she grabbed his arm and pulled him behind her, he didn't have much of a choice. He let the ogre lead him out of the small, wooden hut and into another one. She sat him down on a rough-hewn chair. He leaned his head on his hands and rubbed his eyes while she fussed with whatever concoction she brewed on her crooked wood stove.

A few minutes later, she shoved a hot mug into his hands. "Drink this. It will help with pain and the dizziness."

"I've been advised not to eat or drink any of the food or liquid in the Dark Lands." Wayne eyed it with no small amount of suspicion, the pungent steam making his eyes water, and he pushed it away. "What is it?"

"An herbal tea made with some medicinal plants you wouldn't know if I showed them to you." She pushed it more toward his face. "This is safe for you to drink, so down the hatch. I keep a wide variety of ingredients here in case Light Siders come. The chief will want to see you soon, and you'll need your wits about you."

"I demand you show me the boy, Odara," a voice bellowed from outside. "I wish to see my brother's outcast son for myself."

"Well, he sure didn't wait long, did he?" Wayne frowned, then gulped down the tea and gagged as the bitter brew churned in his stomach. "Why does everyone call me 'boy'? It sounds like an insult, and I don't know how to take it. I choose to believe you don't mean to insult me."

"In ogre years, you're still a child." She opened the door and beckoned him to come out. "Chief Argus has called for you, and he does not like to be kept waiting."

He stood, surprised at how much better he felt. The ogre woman, Odara, must be the healer in this village.

He stepped out into the weak sunlight and hopped on one foot after a sharp stone poked his heel. What he wouldn't give for a decent pair of shoes right now. He'd also love to have his jeans and a better shirt. The colder air outside the hut made him shiver harder, and he wrapped his arms around his waist. *My kingdom for a jacket. And pants. And socks and shoes.*

He looked at the sky. Could he call such a dark sky morning? The weak sun, the reddish-purple sky, and the black trees and foliage made it look more like midnight. The sun told him the day had started no matter what the rest of the light said. However, he could still see the rainbow, even though its light had dulled. He marched up to the chief and winced as he stepped on another rock and glared at him. If the ogres lived in the Old West, he'd definitely earn the title "tenderfoot."

Chief Argus had to be the largest ogre in the village. His leather pants were held up by a length of thick rope. His boots came up to his knees and were spattered with dots of liquid other than mud. He wore a dirty green shirt with loose laces up the front. Around his shoulders he wore a fur cloak, and a crown of twigs sat crooked over his heavy, thick brow.

Wayne folded his arms and stood his ground. *Show no fear*, he reminded himself. "Is there a reason you had me kidnapped?"

Argus towered over him and stared down. "I have reasons for all I do. I am Chief Argus." He snatched up Wayne and crushed him in a tight hug as his feet dangled a good two feet off the ground. "It is good to have you returned home to us, nephew."

Wayne struggled to push himself out of the chief's embrace and staggered back when his feet hit the ground.

"You could have asked in a nicer way. If I'm your nephew, this means you handed over your own brother to the Huntsman to save your life." He took a deep breath and needed to say what he held in his heart. "I told the one ogre who found me in Garland Falls you aren't my chief. I have no tribe. I won't belong to anyone who destroyed my family. I'm sorry if this sounds rude, but you need to know why I don't want to be here."

"I did what needed to be done to ensure the safety of my people. Yes, I handed your father over to the Huntsman, but for the greater good of the tribe. The Huntsman would have taken us all if I hadn't." The chief stared at the ground. "Your father was descended from a long line of ogres who had never been welcomed into the tribe. The whole branch of the family could pass for human. All of them were outcasts, which made your father one as well."

Wayne rubbed his arms as the cold penetrated deeper, down to his bones. "And you thought this a good enough reason to turn your back on him?"

The chief shook his head. "I admit I envied him his ability to come and go to the Light Side lands whenever he wanted. We had a huge argument, and I told him his antics put the whole tribe in danger. After our fight, the tribal elders made him the logical choice for the Huntsman to take. I made a foolish and regrettable mistake when I agreed to the pact."

"Foolish is the least of what I'd call it. You committed a heinous act on your own selfish behalf and the tribe's." Argus' words had the ring of truth, but he wasn't ready to let him off the hook just yet. "Why didn't you try to stop the Huntsman? You could've asked the other tribes to come to your aid." When the chief glanced back at him, Wayne shrugged. "I've studied the lore. There are other tribes, aren't there?"

"Yes, there are other tribes, but none of us interact with each other. Too many ogres together, well, it has never been a very good idea."

"Then maybe ogre law and relations need to change. Look, siblings fight, but then they apologize. So because he looked human, he didn't deserve your forgiveness?" Wayne folded his arms and refused to budge when the chief stepped closer. "Did you hate him when he married a Light Sider?"

Argus glared at him and after a moment looked away before he turned back to him. "You look like your father, but I see the spark of your mother in your eyes. You have his strength of spirit in you, too. His choice of life partner didn't sit well with the chief at the time. He feared your mother's power. Her high rank in her leprechaun clan made him nervous."

"So the tribe betrayed him because of his marriage." He stared at the chief, and his gaze didn't waver for an instant. "After my mother's death, he didn't have a moment's peace. You could've come to him then. You could've been the brother he needed. I need to know why you didn't try to help him."

Argus stood quietly for a long time. "You must understand, the laws of our land were different back then. There were other forces in play at the time. Forces we had no control over. Even though he was my brother, your father had been an outcast all his life. I couldn't defend him forever. He could come and go to the mortal world as much as he pleased. We couldn't." He gestured to himself and Odara. "As you can see, ogres aren't a very handsome lot. I had been forbidden to help when he left our lands."

Wayne turned his back to the chief and stared at Odara. "I may not know everything about ogre law, but I'll tell you this. I know you can't force me to stay here. You talk about a power I have and you need. Well, any power I carry in me is mine and mine alone. Until you can give me a reason, and I mean a solid reason for why you need my help, I can't stay here."

Argus laid a huge hand on Wayne's shoulder. The weight of it almost dropped him to the ground. "You are my last blood relation. It is your duty to use whatever gifts you possess to help your tribe. Let me show you the reason why we need you and it here." He gestured to the crowd that had gathered close. "Come, meet your people."

Wayne hadn't noticed how many of the ogres had gathered around him. He could see them eyeing him with suspicion. Would the chief tell them to welcome him or attack? He hoped it would be the first option.

A small ogre girl, her red hair dancing around her head in the small breeze, tugged on his pants. "Did you for real fight the Huntsman and live?"

He held her hand. "I did. I'm still here, and I can talk to you, can't I?" He grinned when she nodded. "Then I did live through the encounter."

Other children surrounded him and fired questions faster than he could answer them. When the children wouldn't let him leave anytime soon, he sat on the ground and gestured for them to do the same. He reached under his thigh and threw another rock away. Coins jingled in his pockets, and he reached in to pull out a large handful. As more children gathered, he handed them out. The joy on their faces made him smile wider and wider.

The children hung on his every word while he told them how he'd defeated the Huntsman. Then he talked about where he'd grown up and where he lived now. They were more fun to talk to than Chief Argus. No matter what the chief said, forgiveness would come a long time down the road, if ever. As he talked to the children, he had to admit he would defend these little ones to the best of his ability whenever they needed him.

He spied an ogre boy sitting outside the circle by himself. He waved and held his hand out. As the boy approached, the other children moved aside to let him pass.

"How come you're all the way over there by yourself?"

The boy twisted his rough-hewn shirt in his fingers. "I'm different. I'm not supposed to get close to the others."

Wayne studied him and noticed he didn't have the heavy brow and leathery skin as the other children. This boy was made an outcast like his family. Wayne's heart shattered as he thought about the life this child had before him. He patted the ground next to him.

"You guys don't mind if he joins us, do you?" When the children shook their heads or lifted their shoulders, Wayne knew he could change the attitudes by starting with the children. Kids were always more ready to accept those who were different than adults. "Great. Now let's get back to the stories. Do you have any you want to tell?"

Children raised their hands, and he enjoyed listening to them talk about their lives and was sure their parents would be highly embarrassed if they heard the tales coming out of those tiny mouths. These kids were the reason he'd come back here. If they needed him, he'd return no matter what. Eleanor would love these little guys, and he couldn't wait to bring her here.

Chapter Twelve

"Dad." Eleanor ran through her home in the Dark Lands, Hildegard hard on her heels. "Dad, where are you?"

The Ferryman opened his study door, and Eleanor ran into his arms.

"What's wrong, my dear? Tell me what has happened."

As soon as Eleanor returned to her father's house, she reverted back to her skeletal form. She couldn't even give in to the tears threatening to spill because skeletons didn't have the ability to cry. "The ogres have taken Wayne. I need to get him back. What will they do to him? Has Mom seen what happened to him in her visions? They haven't hurt him yet, have they?"

"Your mother hasn't mentioned Wayne to me." He squeezed her one more time and then stepped back. "If he were in danger, she would've known almost immediately. Those visions are the ones she gets on a regular basis."

Hildegard stood nearby with a handkerchief clutched in her hands. "I'm so sorry, Master Ferryman. I failed to protect him as you charged me to do."

The Ferryman turned to the gnome. "Hildegard, you were supposed to keep him company. I didn't expect you to fight anyone. Whereas I know you have some battle skills, I know you don't use them often. I didn't expect you to be a warrior. You've done what I asked of you. You don't need to apologize."

"Dad, he hasn't got the right clothes for the Dark Lands." She held up Wayne's jacket. "I have his invitation and his return key here. If he's in trouble, he has no way to prove he has permission to be there or any way to get home."

The Ferryman took the jacket from Eleanor and turned his sightless gaze to it. "This is serious. The Dark Landers will sense his Light Side blood. They won't tolerate his presence there, but he should be safe for now with the ogres."

"But the ogres are the ones who handed him and his father over to the Huntsman." She walked to the window, but the easy drift of the River of Souls gave her no peace this time. If she'd had a heart, it would skip beats as she considered what the ogres planned. "I have to find him and get him back to Garland Falls, no matter what."

"I understand." The Ferryman stood next to her, and they watched the river creep along its destined path. "You aren't powerless here. Use your abilities to find him. Yes, he has Dark Land blood, but he also carries the Light Side. He'll shine to your soul sight. I know you'll find him."

"I'll go with her, master." Hildegard drew herself up to her full four-foot height. "I shall find Master Wayne and keep him safe."

"I know you will." He walked over to her and laid his bony hand on her shoulder. "You're a faithful servant, Hildegard. I don't know what we'd do without you."

The gnome smiled and bowed to her master. "You will never have to find out."

Eleanor walked over. "We'd better pack what we need. I don't want him in the hands of the ogres any longer than necessary."

Hildegard pulled a small, black bag about the size of a backpack out of the closet. "Let's go retrieve Master Wayne. I'm sure he's in terrible trouble."

"You're right." Eleanor shoved items into the bag. "He may need us sooner than we think."

****

Chief Argus pulled Wayne to his feet and handed him a thick, wooden staff. "Since you will remain with the tribe, you must learn how to defend yourself."

Wayne frowned at the chief and held the staff at his side. "I don't need to learn to defend myself because I'm going back to Garland Falls. As much as I love the children here, I'm not quite ready to forgive you yet. I don't think I ever will be."

"Nephew…"

"My name is Wayne. Please stop claiming me as one of your own. I've had to deal with a lot because of what you cost me. It's going to take some time to get over." He shoved the staff back at the chief. "I suggest you keep your staff and train someone else to use it. I'm out of here as soon as I can find the right door."

"You have no idea what your actions will do." Argus gestured to the woods, a silent and dark guardian. "The creatures who live in the Dark Lands will sense the light in you, boy. Without the protection of the tribe, you won't make it very far."

"I guess it's a chance I'll have to take." He gazed around the small ogre village. "I'm sorry, Chief Argus, but I don't want to stay any longer than necessary."

Wayne headed for the edge of the woods when

Odara stopped him.

"You aren't prepared for what waits for you out there. Your Light Side blood will be a beacon to those who wish to harm you. You'll not be able to hide your presence from them for very long." She pushed him toward her home. "Come with me. I'll see you have better protection than your current garb. Your feet will be cut to ribbons on the trails out of the Dark Lands."

Wayne walked ahead of her into her home and sat while she rummaged in a large trunk. Once again, nausea boiled up in his stomach to burn his throat. The last time he felt like this had been when the ogre confronted him in the park. How many more times would this illness cripple him? He'd laugh if he turned out to be allergic to ogres. That meant he'd make himself sick.

He rubbed his forehead and frowned. His face and his fingers didn't feel right. Had they changed again? If so, what made this keep happening, and could he stop it? He swore if this was his bad leprechaun luck, he would give up right now. The nausea eased, and he blew out a breath. Finally, he started to feel better.

"Do you have a mirror? Something's wrong with my face. I want to see if I got punched in it."

She handed him a silver hand mirror with a cloudy glass. He held it up and studied his features. The ogre from the park had said he shapeshifted, and from what he was seeing, he had. He still looked like himself, but the classic Hollywood good looks people told him he possessed had disappeared. His light-brown hair had turned shaggy, and the color faded to a mud brown. His brow protruded over his eyes, and his nose had elongated and hooked under at the end. At least it wasn't allergies. Once again, the silver lining showed up.

"What's happened to me?" His hands had increased in size as well as his arms, shoulders, and his torso. His legs thickened, and he bumped his head on the ceiling when he shot to his feet. "How could I have shapeshifted and into an ogre? Odara, do you know what could be the cause of this?"

The ogre walked around him and studied him from all angles. "I have no explanation for why your features and stature have altered this way. I don't know of any creature to make such a drastic change in their appearance."

"This didn't have to do with your crazy tea, did it?" He had to smile. "If so, can you make more to turn me back to normal?"

"No, boy." She turned back to the stove and cackled. "I wouldn't know how to make a potion to do this. Maybe it's your leprechaun blood. They're known to be shapeshifters."

"No, they aren't." Wayne looked at his face in the mirror. "They're said to be tricksters and play pranks. And please don't call me 'boy' any longer. I'm a man in my thirties."

"As you wish." Odara plopped some items on the table and handed a book to him. "Read more of the lore of your people. There are many races of leprechauns, like ogres, fairies, and humans. It appears your mother had some shapeshifter blood in her and passed it along to you."

"I changed like this before when the other ogre confronted me in Garland Falls." He laid the mirror on the table. "Will I be able to control it?"

"Those are questions for the leprechauns, not ogres." She turned and handed him a burlap sack. "There are some provisions in here for you. I said I keep Light Sider food here. What you've been told is right. Don't eat any of the Dark Lands food. It will hamper your return to the mortal world." She eyed him. "You need better travel clothes than your current garb."

"Why do you want to help me, Odara? The chief wants me to stay here, and you've almost pushed me out the door."

She stood straight but kept her bent back to him. "Your father and I were friends. We grew up together and got up to all sorts of trouble. The chief at the time disapproved of your family, but I didn't care. I fought to stop his banishment, but my family made me be silent when they voted with the tribe to have him traded for the safety of our people."

Wayne walked over to her and laid his now overly large hand on her shoulder. "Thank you for your friendship to him." When she turned to look at him, he smiled. "And for your friendship to me."

"If you are determined to find your way home, I'll help you all I can." She held out some clothes. "I don't know how well this will fit when, or if, you return to your normal appearance. As they say, it is better to have what's at hand than none."

He held the pants up to his waist. "If you've got a belt in case they end up too big, I'd appreciate it. I'm not too worried about the shirt."

She gave him a length of rope and held up a pair of boots. "These might be too large, but you need protection for your feet."

He eyed the boots before he shrugged and bowed to Odara's judgment. He couldn't hike through the woods with no protection. He pulled on the clothes over his shorts and T-shirt. She raised her bushy eyebrows, and he grinned. "I refuse to leave one piece of me behind in this village."

"Odara, I wish to see the boy again." At the chief's bellow, they looked at each other.

"Great." Wayne rolled his eyes as Odara chuckled. "His Majesty calls."

He pushed open the door and stepped outside. Could it still be daytime? Had twilight begun to fall? Who could tell when the sky looked the same all the time? He stared at his rainbow and frowned when it faded a little more. He didn't want to talk to Argus any longer. The chief was bound to make him stay in the village, and he'd consider it if Eleanor could be here with him.

"Whatever you want to tell me, make it quick." Wayne scanned the assembled crowd. "I guess the whole tribe wants to hear what you have to say."

Argus towered over Wayne, but he refused to step back. He'd never shown weakness in his life and didn't plan to start now. Even though the ogre could crush him without a second thought. The two eyed each other while the ogres looked on. He almost stumbled from the weight of the tension between them.

"I demand you stay in the village, boy."

Wayne laughed. "Are you serious? I can't stay here. My life is in the mortal world, and I wish to return there. I have friends and a woman who I believe has started to love me. I will get back there. I'd like to have your help to return, but if you won't, I'll manage on my own. I plan to leave, and you can't stop me."

Argus scowled and grabbed Wayne's shirt. "Oh, can't I?"

He pulled Wayne along after him to a small hut

behind the village. He opened the door and threw him inside. "You'll stay here, boy, until you come to your senses. I'll not be disrespected by someone like you. You may be next to sit as chief, but I'm the chief now, and you'll do as you're told."

Wayne flinched as the door slammed shut. "So much for my great plan to leave as soon as I could. Now what the heck do I do?" He sat on the floor and hung his head. And here he'd thought his situation couldn't get any worse. "Where's that silver lining now, genius? Yeah, you make magic with numbers, but all the other magic people say you have? Well, it'd be nice if it showed up right about now."

Chapter Thirteen

The sun sank low in the reddish-purple sky as Eleanor stared out over the gnarled trees and rocky hills of the Dark Lands. With the sky turning darker, she knew a storm would hit at any time. And mortals thought their weather was unpredictable. She shouldered the pack and smiled down at Hildegard when the gnome patted her hand. Thank goodness Hildegard had decided to come with her.

"I'm glad to have some company on this journey. I don't think I'd have the heart or the nerve if I had to do this alone."

"Some of the jobs you think might be the hardest to do may be the easiest to complete, mistress."

"How will we to find him, Hildegard?" Eleanor's shoulders slumped as she looked around. He'd been gone for hours and who knew how far he'd been dragged off to. "The ogres could have taken him anywhere."

"I know, mistress, but we can't give up. Yes, the ogres have a huge realm, but as soon as we enter, your soul sight should be able to pick up a faint trace of him." Hildegard smiled at Eleanor. "We shall have Master Wayne back with us before you know it."

"Dad's right." She shouldered the bag a little higher as they set off. "I don't know what we'd do without you."

"Hush now, mistress. I do my job, and I happen to love to take care of you and your family." She winked.

"And I love my conversations with Master Wayne. He tells such wonderful stories."

As they set off away from the Ferryman's castle, Eleanor glanced at the gnome. "I didn't know Wayne told you stories. What are they about?"

"He tells me about his time, as he calls it, back east. He's some kind of money changer from what I gather."

Eleanor laughed. "He's an accountant. He helps people keep track of their expenses and how to save their hard-earned money."

"Money and its problems confuse me, mistress." They walked on a little farther before Hildegard spoke again. "You don't think the ogres have hurt him, do you?"

"I don't think so. My mother would have told me if she'd seen any bad omens." Eleanor stepped over a small boulder and helped the gnome climb over it. "I think for right now, he's okay. Let's hope we find him before his situation changes."

Eleanor had another worry she didn't want to mention to Hildegard. Even the gnome's positive outlook wouldn't dispel this fear. She looked at her bony, skeletal hands. How would Wayne react when he found out her flesh-and-blood self was only a pretense? Would he still want her as a skeleton? Even if he accepted her, could they have a future together?

The Dark Lands always revealed one's true appearance. She didn't want to lose Wayne, but she needed him to be safe and returned to Garland Falls unharmed. This mattered more than her own fears of her appearance. Maybe it would turn out all right. She sighed as they walked on. He had warned her his leprechaun luck sabotaged his personal life on an almost constant basis.

"What troubles you, mistress?"

"Too many thoughts of how much could go wrong."

Hildegard stopped and put her hands on her hips. "I need you to do better, mistress. I've known you since you were a baby. Now tell me what's the matter."

"This." Eleanor raised her hand, and her sleeve slid down to reveal her skeletal arm. "How will Wayne feel about me when he finds out I'm a skeleton? And not any skeleton either. I'm the daughter of the Ferryman who takes souls to the underworld."

The gnome stood silent as she rubbed her chin. "I think he'll see the value in a lower grocery bill." She grinned when Eleanor laughed. "But you only revert to a skeleton just when you reside in the Dark Lands. You're flesh and blood in the mortal world."

Eleanor threw her arms around her friend. "You always know what to say to make me feel better. I guess I'll find out when the time comes. Let's go."

At times, Eleanor hated the fact her father's house sat away from any town or village. At other times, she loved the fact she and her parents weren't crowded on top of all the other residents. She planned to stop at a small cabin at the halfway mark, since she'd gotten a late start. If her luck held, she shouldn't have any problems.

****

Wayne kicked the door again and again but got no result. The ogres sure knew how to build their structures. He had no option but to stay put until someone came to let him out. He sat on the floor and thumped his head against the wall. He'd suffered through the weird stuff with doors changing colors. He'd been threatened by an ogre in a contemporary town. Yes, the town had magic, but what the heck? How had he gotten into this mess in the first place? He'd been kidnapped and, somehow, changed into an ogre. The one bright spot in this magical soap opera was Eleanor.

He smiled when he thought of her. With her black hair and blue eyes, she'd been the one sane moment in the whole situation. He loved her company and had watched as she talked with her customers. She had a great love for books. Then Hildegard had shown up, and he'd grown used to her presence faster than he thought possible. Would he see either of them again?

If he could sleep, maybe he could talk briefly with the Ferryman's daughter and she could get a message to Eleanor or Hildegard. "The thing is, do I want to take the chance?" he muttered.

The light in the small hut dimmed, and he got up to peek through the cracks between the wooden slats. Looked like the sun had started to set. Great. This would have been the perfect time to escape the ogre village. He plopped back down onto the floor. Might as well try to get some rest while he could. Who knew what would happen the next day? As he started to drift off, the door opened, and he jumped to his feet.

Odara threw a sack at him. "You have to leave now, or Argus will never let you."

He hefted the sack and stared at her. "Why does he want to keep me here so much?"

"He's afraid of you, boy." She hobbled over to him and held his hands. "You carry a strong, magical power in you. If you learn to control it, he fears you would harm the Dark Lands and his tribe. It's why he can't let you leave."

"How ridiculous can he get? The little I know about

what I can do isn't worth worrying about." He grew silent for a second or two. The doors that changed and opened for him could be considered a power. He didn't even want to mention the rainbow that followed him. "He doesn't have to worry. I wouldn't hurt anyone here, no matter how angry I get at him. Even if I'm not a fan of his, I don't wish harm to happen to the children or anyone else here."

She shook her head and gripped his hands tighter. "The Light Siders will sense your presence and come for you if you grow stronger." She opened the door and peered in both directions. "You must go now. There is a trail behind this cabin. Follow it. It will take you to the Light Side. The leprechaun clans should help you get back home."

He stepped out the door and gave Odara a quick tight hug. "Thank you. You're a good friend, and I'm lucky to have you in my life."

She smiled and patted his back before she pushed him toward the path he needed to take. While he hugged the shadows, she stayed behind him. Wayne eased his way to the back of the cabin and gave her one last nod. Then he gripped the provisions bag and ran into the dark woods and never looked back.

****

"We'll stop here for the night." Eleanor glanced around their temporary shelter.

The wooden floor had started to warp in places, giving the whole place the illusion of rolling waves. Tall weeds with black flowers and long thorns grew between the wide cracks. Mildew clung to the ceiling more than the chipped paint did. The broken windows let in the cool night air, but not enough to banish the damp, musty smell permeating the room. She couldn't even light a fire for Hildegard as most of the stones from the fireplace littered the floor.

She looked around and placed her hands on her hips. "This place looks worse every time I come here." She shook her head as she kicked debris out of her way. "I wish someone cared enough to fix it up. I'd do it, but I don't have the time, and my father wouldn't let me anyway. Travelers need a safe place to rest. Maybe I can talk him into finding someone later on to do it."

Hildegard tiptoed in behind her and frowned. "You have come here often, mistress? I don't think it's a good idea for you to be here, especially on your own."

Eleanor shut the door and set the bag down by one of the chairs. The cushion sagged almost to the floor, and she adjusted herself, but she couldn't find a comfortable position. "It's a convenient stop when I have to run errands for Dad or when I need to visit some of the other residents of the Dark Lands. For all its awful looks, this cabin is a safe place. Please eat your dinner. We should be at the ogres' village tomorrow. Let's hope the first one we check is the right one."

"I believe it will be, mistress. Your soul sight wouldn't lead you in the wrong direction." Hildegard pulled out a small hunk of bread, cheese, and some fruit. "I hope Master Wayne hasn't eaten any Dark Land food."

"I'm sure he hasn't. After all, Lucas and Parker Callahan warned him." She settled herself a little more into the chair, and her knees rose almost to her top rib. "Of course, he didn't expect to be taken in the middle of the night."

Hildegard nodded and finished her light supper. She

pulled her cloak tighter around her shoulders and curled up in the only other chair in the room. "Good night, mistress. We'll find Master Wayne tomorrow. I'm sure."

As her friend settled in for the night, Eleanor kept her fears to herself. The ogres had to know of Wayne's heritage, but why take him? What could they want with him? Could he be more important to the tribe than anyone knew? She tried to rest, but her worries and fears rattled around in her bony skull. They had to find Wayne before some evil befell him.

She sat back and prayed for the night to end soon. They needed to get back on the search for the man who spoke to her living and unliving heart, quicker than she'd believed.

Chapter Fourteen

Eleanor sat up the next morning, still exhausted. She'd gotten very little rest. She stretched, and her spine cracked as she arched her back. "Last night was one of those nights I wish I could sleep like mortals. If so, I could've taken a tonic to knock myself out. No rest means a long day."

"Your back sounds bad, mistress." Hildegard looked up from her breakfast. "I watched you toss and turn most of the night. I know the furniture here isn't comfortable, but I'm sure the lack of comfort didn't contribute to your restlessness."

"You know me way too well, Hildegard." She walked to the window. This habit had become more and more prevalent of late. She'd never been one to stare out windows before, but now if there was a window, she could be found in front of it. "We'll be at the ogre village today. I hope Wayne is there and we can take him with us."

The gnome handed her the bag. "Mistress, you are the Ferryman's daughter. Your word carries as much weight as anyone's in the Dark Lands hierarchy. The ogre chief must do as you say."

They stepped outside and continued down the trail.

"It would work in a perfect world, Hildegard. However, this world is far from perfect." Eleanor glanced at the sky and stopped. "Do you see what I see?

Look."

"A rainbow?" Hildegard frowned before she turned to Eleanor. "How is this possible? Rainbows never appear in the Dark Lands. They're usually contained by the boundaries of the Light Side. At least I've never heard of rainbows in the Dark Lands."

The two women stared at the sky. Never in all the years in the Dark Lands had a bright, colorful rainbow appeared. It arced into the distance and pulsated with an almost impossible glow.

Eleanor laid a hand over her mouth. "It has to be a sign Wayne is still unhurt. We'll follow the rainbow, and maybe he'll be at the other end. Come on. I'm sure this will lead us to where he waits for us."

Hildegard grinned from ear to ear. "Maybe Master Wayne will be your treasure at the end."

"You might be right, Hildegard. You very well might be right."

Eleanor broke into a trot, Hildegard hard on her heels.

****

Wayne sat on a black stump and pulled off his boots as he tried to ignore the sharp stabs of splinters into his backside. Yep. He grimaced when he saw his feet. Blisters had broken out on the tops, the bottoms, and the backs of his ankles. Even though he still had the features and the size of an ogre, the clothes and boots rubbed his skin raw. He would have loved to have gotten the thick ogre skin to go with his shapeshifted form. How much longer until he could find someone to help him return to Garland Falls? If he had his return key, he could've gone back last night.

He looked at the path he followed and shuddered.

"No way could I walk on whatever those thorny plants are." His gaze shot to the underbrush. The scurrying of unseen creatures gave him less confidence. "Those black, twisted trees have ripped me up something fierce. If it weren't for the clothes Odara gave me, I'd be in a lot worse shape than a few blisters. Now, I've got to start the climb over these boulders."

He pulled on his boots and stood. "I hope the Light Side lands aren't too much farther down this trail. This whole trip has been a lot more than I expected." He adjusted the too big clothes and started walking again. "I just want to get back to Garland Falls and wear something that actually fits me. Of course, my bigger problem is how do I look like myself again? Argus was right about one thing. Ogres are not a handsome race."

He missed his cell phone almost as much as he missed thick, comfy socks. "I wish I could call for a ride. Magic is okay, but traveling here without any means to call someone is hard on the feet." He stared at the sky, happy to see the bright colors against the Dark Lands' reddish-purple sky. "At least I still have the rainbow near me."

He stood and reached out his hand. The light appeared close enough to touch. As he stretched out, the different colors drifted down to swirl around his fingers. He watched the light caress his hand and wrap around his body. The different colors warmed him, and his aches and pains lessened a little. He lifted his hand again, and the light traveled up his arm to return to the sky.

He limped down the trail and kept an eye on the rainbow. "This has to be a good sign, right?" As he moved down the trail, the colorful light appeared to follow him. "Hey, if this beautiful sign of hope likes me, my personal luck has to be changing for the better. Now if the rainbow would heal my feet, I'll be in great shape."

His one-sided conversation ended when he was hit from behind and fell to the ground.

****

Chief Argus bowed deeply to Eleanor, his hand over his heart. "We didn't expect a visit from the Ferryman's daughter, Mistress Eleanor. How are your mother and father?"

Eleanor stood tall as she gazed at the chief. "They are well, thank you, Chief Argus."

"And why do you honor our humble village this day?"

"I'm on the search for someone. His name is Wayne Billings, and I had word your ogres brought him here. Where is he, Chief?" She leaned close. "And please don't lie. I can see signs he has been here. So tell me his location."

Argus bowed deeper. "I don't know, ma'am. We had given him shelter for the night, but he disappeared long after the village retired to their beds."

Eleanor called up her soul sight. His light shone in the middle of the village, in the cabin behind her, and led to another small hut at the edge of the woods. She straightened her back as she marched over to the cabin. Wayne's light shone brightest here, so this must have been the last place he stayed.

She opened the door and stepped inside. The door had no handle on this side, and the room barely had enough space for one person to fit in. Argus could call it a cabin all he wanted, but it felt more like a jail.

She whirled around and stared at the chief. "What happened to Wayne?"

"I don't know, ma'am." He shrank back and held his hands up. "I requested he stay in here, and then he disappeared."

She stalked over to where the chief cowered at her feet. "Pray I find him soon, Chief Argus. If I discover you have harmed him in any way, I shall be most upset. Don't make me come back here." She glanced at the gnome. "Come along, Hildegard. This ogre has been a waste of our time."

As she walked around to the back of the cabin, Odara met her there. "Mistress Eleanor, may I speak with you?"

"What is it?" she snapped. She'd had enough of ogres and wanted to get back on the search for Wayne. "I'm sorry. I'm just worried about him. Tell me what you know."

Odara looked around and lowered her voice. "I helped your man escape. Chief Argus would never have let him leave. Argus fears the powerful magic Wayne carries in him. I told him how to get to the Light Side. I hope you find him there."

Eleanor stared at the woods. "I hope I do, too. Thank you for the help you gave him."

She and Hildegard set off at a trot. Eleanor wanted to get away from the ogres as fast as possible. The sounds from the village faded, and they slowed their pace.

"Hildegard, how close are we to the Light Side?"

"Not close enough." The gnome breathed heavily as she walked a few paces ahead. "We should be at the brownies' village before dark. Maybe they know of Master Wayne's location."

"I hope so. He doesn't have provisions or decent clothes. The Dark Lands are not kind to the unprepared."

She shook her head. "If he'd been able to take his return key and the invitation, we wouldn't be so afraid for him."

"True, but the best we can do now is find Master Wayne. Don't forget he is resourceful. He can talk his way out of most situations. He told me his skills in speaking are beyond compare." Hildegard straightened her shoulders and held out her hand. "Come, mistress. Wayne waits for us to find him, and look. The rainbow has gotten brighter. I believe we're closer to him than ever."

"You're right. It didn't shine this bright before. We need to hurry."

Eleanor couldn't believe how far Wayne had come. She'd see footprints in the dirt, and her soul sight showed the light he left behind. She knew Wayne had passed this way, but how long ago? They had walked close to an hour before the gnome pulled her to a stop.

"Mistress, look." Hildegard pointed to the sky. "The rainbow's light has dimmed. What do you think it means?"

"There might be the possibility he's been hurt or maybe more Dark Landers have taken him."

Hildegard glanced around and poked behind rocks and fallen trees. "I don't see any indication of injury, but it might have happened farther down the road. Let's hurry. Master Wayne needs our help quicker than we believed."

Eleanor shouldered the bag and forced herself to keep a pace comfortable for Hildegard. However, she wanted to run down the narrow trail to find Wayne. The gnome huffed and puffed behind her, and she slowed her pace even more. "I'm sorry, Hildegard. I keep forgetting your shorter legs have trouble keeping up with me and I don't tire as quickly as you do."

"Don't worry, mistress. The exercise is good for me." The gnome pointed to the ground and stooped down for a closer look. "Master Wayne must have been ambushed right here."

Eleanor turned her gaze to the surrounding woods. "I believe you're right."

Hildegard turned to her left. "The drag marks go off in this direction. Mistress, it appears the brownies have taken him."

Eleanor couldn't stop the groan that escaped. Brownies didn't live in the Dark Lands or on the Light Side. They were given a small parcel of land, provided they stayed away from both lands. If the brownies did have Wayne, this would be harder than she thought to get him back. They lived by scavenger rules. If they found any item or even a person, they kept it. She and Hildegard carried no trinket to bargain with to win his freedom.

"We're all in big trouble."

Hildegard rubbed her arms. "Mistress, you are very right."

****

Wayne moaned, and his eyes fluttered open. He hung over a hole in the ground with a crowd of small people around it. Thick vines dug into his back from the net he swung in high above the ground. The rough vines rubbed his skin raw, even though his clothes gave him some protection. Why would they bind his hands? He obviously couldn't go anywhere or hurt anyone.

A crowd of them pawed through the bag Odara had given him. There went his supplies. He suspected they were brownies by the muted brown and green colors they wore, but he didn't see any weapons. Looked like they enjoyed ambushes so their victims couldn't fight back.

At least his feet didn't hurt right now. Of course that was a small consolation to his current predicament. "Okay, you've had your fun." He yanked on the ropes and swung in a slow circle. "I'm tired of being taken prisoner. You've got my things, so you can now feel free to cut me loose."

One brownie stepped forward and poked his side with a stick. "You will be silent, ogre. Your kind trespasses into our territory all the time, and we won't stand for it any longer."

"What do you mean 'my kind'? I'm not an ogre." He frowned and stared at his bound overly large, ogre-ish-looking hands. "Well, half of me isn't. Look, you people ambushed me. I walked on a public trail and minded my own business. So I couldn't have trespassed into your territory if you brought me here."

The crowd huddled together and murmured while Wayne spun in slow circles above them. After finding out his magical heritage, he'd realized the "normal life" ship had sailed. After all he'd seen and done, would he want to have a normal life again? He pressed his lips together and tried hard not to laugh. Taken prisoner by people half his size.

This has got to be the most ridiculous situation I've ever found myself in.

He caught a few words they said, but their language sounded different. They had some English vocabulary; otherwise, they couldn't have spoken to him. He glanced in their direction and rolled his eyes when they lowered their voices.

"Hey, if you want to talk about me, I have a right to

know what you're saying. So either speak up or be quiet."

The leader poked him again. "You will hush, ogre. We need to decide what to do with you."

"How about you turn me loose so I can get to the Light Side? I want to go home to Garland Falls. Can you give me at least a little cooperation?"

"You go nowhere." The leader thumped the stick on the ground. "We found you, so we get to keep you."

They went back to their huddle and murmured voices while Wayne sighed and shook his head. *Oh, for pity's sake.* First the ogre tribe had tried to hold him, and now these petulant brownies had the same plan. If he'd known everyone here wanted to take him prisoner, he would've stayed in Trenton. Of course he'd find a way out of this mess. But what kind of plan would he come up with, and how on earth could he implement it?

He thought of Eleanor with her beautiful blue eyes and black hair. He'd been drawn to her the first time he saw her. When she was close, he'd swear he felt a little push inside him to keep him close to her. She had said she had her own magical talents. Maybe that was why he couldn't make any relationship work. He needed someone magical, like him.

When Hildegard found he'd been taken, had she run to Eleanor to get help? Did the two of them have the means to try and find him? Even though she'd never said, he felt Eleanor knew the Dark Lands. Hildegard said she worked for the Ferryman. So the gnome had to know her way around here, too, right? He didn't need any more complications than he had right now.

He glanced at the sky and noticed the rainbow's light had dimmed. It must have happened when the brownies clobbered him. He stared at the colorful arc and concentrated on it. As he did, it began to glow brighter again. At least he had the rainbow.

As a leprechaun, he wondered if he would find his own pot of gold at the end. Would that treasure be a future with a certain black-haired bookstore owner? First, he had to get out of this situation. Then get to the Light Side, then home. Why did his plan sound way too easy to work?

Chapter Fifteen

The brownie he'd spoken to wandered over to a thick vine and tugged on it.

Wayne looked up as the net opened and he fell to the ground. "Ow. I've already got a lot of bruises. You didn't need to give me more." He pushed to his feet and held his arms straight out. "How about you finish the job and cut me loose? My wrists are raw from these vines."

"Not until our leader says we can." The little man peered closer at Wayne. "Why don't you look like an ogre any longer? Is this some sort of trick?"

Wayne held his hands up and then felt his forehead. He must look like his normal self again. "It's not a trick, I promise. This is a new wrinkle in my life, and I'm still trying to understand it. You have my word I'm not here to harm you or anyone else."

A brownie woman, a little taller than the rest of her people, strode out of a large house and stopped in front of him. "I am Elder Rikka, leader of this brownie hamlet. You will explain your purpose for your travels through our lands."

Wayne bowed to the small woman. A show of respect always softened the toughest customer, and Rikka was no exception. At least, he hoped she wasn't an exception. "My name is Wayne Billings. The ogres kidnapped me from Garland Falls, and all I want is to get back there. I didn't mean to trespass in your lands."

"Your pretty words may sound true, but I suspect they are false." She walked around him and poked him with her staff at odd intervals. "We don't know what you are, and you make us suspicious. You looked like an ogre when you first arrived. Now you carry more human features. Explain yourself."

He glanced around at the brownies as they stared at him and whispered among themselves. "I wish I could give you the answers you want. These changes started in the ogre village. I promise you I'm not a full ogre. I'm half leprechaun also."

The brownies jumped away from him as though he'd claimed kinship with the devil incarnate. Their voices grew louder, and mothers shielded their children from him. The crowd shrank back, and several brownies ran and hid. The first brownie who'd spoken to him grabbed his bound hands and dragged him down to his knees.

Rikka held her hands up, and the crowd quieted down. "Leprechauns and ogres can't be trusted. I suspect you have some nefarious purpose in our lands."

"Believe me or don't." His patience had started to run out. "Look, I'm tired, I'm hungry, and I want to get back to where I came from. That's all."

"Don't believe him, Elder." The brownie who'd poked him first came forward with his stick pointed at Wayne's chest. "If he's related to the leprechauns, he's an enemy of the brownies."

"Put him where he can't cause any trouble until I decide how to handle him." She turned to the crowd. "Elders, if you will all come with me?"

The first brownie pulled hard, and Wayne stumbled to his feet.

"You will remain locked up until Elder Rikka decides what to do with you."

He gave Wayne a hard shove into a small hut, then slammed the door in his face.

Wayne looked around the small room and shook his head. "Here we go again, but at least this time there's furniture in here."

A small table with two chairs sat in the middle of the tiny room. He straightened up and banged his head on the low ceiling. He eyed the chairs and knew they couldn't hold his weight. He didn't need broken furniture to make them even more suspicious. The floor looked to be his only option.

He rattled the door on its hinges. "This thing doesn't look too sturdy. I can probably knock it down with a couple of kicks."

He crawled over to the window and watched the brownies. They threw logs into the pit he'd hung over and pointed to his makeshift jail.

"This does not look good for me. They couldn't want to eat me, could they?"

He crawled over to the back wall and pushed on it. He grinned as it bent under his shoulder. He pushed harder, and it fell to the ground with a quiet thud. "Sorry, my little friends, but the time has come for me to go."

As he ran into the woods, he glanced up at the rainbow. "Well, rainbow, if you could lead me to the Light Side, I'd really appreciate any help you can give me. I have no provisions and no idea how much farther I need to go." Gold coins clinked together in his pocket as he ran. "I need help, not more coins. However, I can at least pay for any assistance if I need to."

He started down the narrow trail, and the ropes fell

off his wrists. His pants sagged down around his hips, and he tripped over the boots now three sizes too large. The shirt he wore hung down to his knees. He fished around in his pants pocket and found the thin rope Odara had given him. As he tied his pants up, he glanced at the trees that lined the path. They'd been tall before, but now they towered over him.

"Why do the trees and the rest of the forest look bigger now?"

He held his hands up. The skin had turned brown and leathery. His hands were also a lot smaller than when he'd been taken prisoner. His smaller stature confirmed what happened when he shapeshifted to an ogre. His body had changed again.

"Am I ever going to get used to this or learn more control? At least I'm not nauseous or dizzy this time. I don't have Odara to help me. Maybe I'm learning how this works and what to do."

He trotted down the path, stepping around rocks and branches. "Okay, so I'm a brownie now. And my clients were confused by tax season. At least they didn't have to deal with this."

He grinned as he hurried away from the brownies' hamlet.

****

Eleanor and Hildegard arrived in the brownie hamlet as the flames in the pit grew higher. A net made of vines lay on the ground next to it. Eleanor looked around the village with her soul sight. Sure enough, Wayne had been here, his light brighter than before. She glanced up at the rainbow. Its light shone bright against the lavender twilight sky.

"What do you mean you planned to cook him?"

Hildegard stared at Rikka. "Have you lost what little sense you have left, cousin?"

"You will watch your tone with me, Hildegard. You were the one who decided a life of servitude would suit you better than your heritage."

"Bah. I like the life I've chosen. I'd rather clean all day, every day than listen to your complaints for the rest of my life."

Eleanor stepped between the two of them. In all her years of Hildegard's time in her home, she'd never once seen the gnome lose her temper. "Let's all take a deep breath and step back for a moment. Now, where is Wayne so we can return him to the mortal world?"

Rikka pointed to the small hut at the edge of the village by itself. "He's in there, but we found him, so we get to keep him."

"Stop it, Rikka. You can't keep people." Hildegard stepped closer to her cousin. "And you said you wanted to eat him."

"Oh, you know we wouldn't have eaten him. We wanted to scare him so he would tell the truth about himself." Rikka laughed, and she shoved Hildegard back a few paces. "Brownies can keep whatever we deem valuable. The ogre you call Wayne will be a great protector for our hamlet."

Eleanor and Hildegard glanced at each other. "Why do you need protection? Hildegard has told me you are all quick to defend yourselves when necessary."

"True, but there have been more Dark Landers seen outside our hamlet. They are much bigger than us. Our defenses won't protect us from them when they decide to attack."

Hildegard folded her arms and stared at her cousin.

"What did the brownies do this time?"

Rikka shuffled from foot to foot and wouldn't look at Hildegard and kept her gaze from Eleanor. "We may have borrowed a small trinket and forgot to give it back."

"I can't believe you. You have to give back what you stole, and the Dark Landers will go home." The gnome shook her head. "I don't know why anyone in any realm puts up with you. Return the item."

Eleanor laid her bony fingers on Rikka's shoulder. "You have to make this right. Don't make me call the Dark Lands hierarchy into this. If you return the item, no one has to know." She folded her arms and turned her sightless gaze to the brownie elder. "Now, if we've settled your issue, take me to Wayne."

The three of them trooped to the hut, and Rikka flung open the door. She gasped at where the back wall used to be. Eleanor walked over and opened her soul sight again. Wayne had been here and left not long ago. Looked like he made his own escape. She gazed up and smiled at the colorful rainbow as it painted the sky with brilliant colors. She took it as a sign of Wayne's continued good health.

"I believe he refused to be your prisoner any longer." She looked over her shoulder at Rikka. "I'm pretty sure he also had no desire to be eaten or to be your protector. Come on, Hildegard. We should be able to catch up to him soon."

As they jogged down the trail, Eleanor turned to Hildegard. "I want to thank you again for your company."

"Of course, mistress. You know I'll help you and Master Wayne with whatever you need. I will assist you any way I can. You two will make a fine couple once all this is over."

"I'm a skeleton and he's not. How would a relationship this different work?"

Hildegard chuckled. "You aren't a skeleton in Garland Falls, are you?" She waited while her mistress shook her head. "Then live in Garland Falls."

"Hildegard, you know I have a job with my dad to help souls cross over to the afterlife. I can't stay in the mortal world all the time."

The gnome stepped over a rock on the path. "Who said you had to be there all the time? From what I understand, all mortals work more than one job. You could, too, and Wayne could be with you."

"You make a lot of sense. Let's see how he feels when he finds out the woman of his dreams is a pile of bones."

"Believe it will work out fine, mistress." She winked as a smile curled her lips. "I have a sense about these things."

Chapter Sixteen

"Will Eleanor and Hildegard ever find me? That's if they're even looking or know where to look." Wayne winced as he tried to massage the soreness from his feet. "How can such tiny blisters hurt so much? Maybe one day I'll return to the ogre village and give them socks and belts and some softer cloth. Burlap is not good clothing material."

He wanted to go back to the ogres. He'd love to learn more about that half of his life, but by his choice, not theirs. He'd enjoyed the ogre children and their questions. They had a natural curiosity about him, Garland Falls, and the mortal world where he lived. He had to let the past go and try to understand the motives behind making his father an outcast. However, letting go of the past had turned out to be harder than he thought.

He looked to his right down the long path he still had to travel. How would his mother's family react when they saw him? He wanted to learn from the leprechauns also. Based on peoples' reactions to him so far, he didn't hold out much hope. He pushed to his achy and abused feet. He'd find out soon enough. He'd been to two villages and had been thrown in jail in both places. Maybe the third time would be the charm.

The whole situation with the brownies was almost laughable. They were so small and fierce he wanted to believe they'd been kidding about eating him. Then they'd thrown him into that tiny hut, and it hadn't seemed so funny any longer. He was glad he'd gotten out when he did. Maybe if he got to come back here, he'd help them build better homes. His dad had taught him a few things before he became ill.

Right now, all he could think about was Eleanor and his friends. He smiled as he included Hildegard in the list. What he wouldn't give to be in Eleanor's bookstore with a cup of tea. He'd share some of Heavenly Bites' cookies with Hildegard. As much as he enjoyed the gnome's company, Eleanor was the one he wanted to be with. He wasn't sure when, but she'd stolen his heart.

He glanced at the rainbow in the sky, and it looked brighter. Did Renee and Parker miss him yet? He knew he'd been here for at least two days. Miss Dee had to notice he hadn't been down for meals. He crossed his fingers and prayed it hadn't been longer. If he had his return key, he'd be a lot more confident about his current circumstances. Thinking about food made his stomach rumble.

"If I can't get something to eat soon, I'm going to pass out before the end of this trip."

At least he figured out how to get back to his normal size. He no longer carried the features of brownies or ogres. Without a mirror, he had no idea if he'd returned to his normal features. How many more times would his looks change, and could he get control of those strange abilities? He needed someone he could talk to, someone who would understand.

"Eleanor, where are you? Did Hildegard tell you I'd been taken?" His shoulders slumped forward as, for the first time since his father had died, his emotional strength leached away. "I'm stuck in a strange world. I have no food, no decent clothes, my feet are torn up, and I want to get back to Miss Dee's bed-and-breakfast. Plus, now I shapeshift with no clue when or why it will happen. I just want to go back to Garland Falls."

"I guess you're lost?" said a musical voice off to his left.

He whipped around, ready for someone to try and take him prisoner. A small fairy with iridescent wings stood on a leaf. He'd been so wrapped up in his thoughts he never noticed how the landscape changed. Gone were the black, twisted trees. The sky had changed to a pale blue, and the woods looked more like they did in Garland Falls. Of course, he'd never seen purple trees or blue bushes before, but the odd colors and foliage were easier on the eyes than the ones in the Dark Lands.

"You could say I'm lost. I need to get to the Light Side. I hope someone there can help me get back to the mortal world."

The fairy smiled. "I see."

He shivered as the hairs on the back of his neck rose and his skin prickled. "I'd better hit the road. I don't want to keep you from any important business you may have to see to."

"You aren't." The fairy flew around his face. "You don't know the rules of this realm. You can't walk into a fairy's forest and not give any tribute."

Wayne sighed as he laid his head back and rolled his eyes. "Fine. What do you want? I have to say, I'm a little tired of everyone here and their demands I give them some kind of doodad."

"I wish to have a tiny item from you. An item you will never even miss." She leaned close. "A small lock of your hair is all I require."

"I don't believe this. A lock of hair? Are you crazy?"

"I would never tease about tribute. Pay me the toll and have safe passage through our forest."

Crashing in the underbrush made his hands ball into fists as he looked for whatever came through. What or who could be after him this time? All the while the small fairy hovered closer to him and held her hands out, a malicious grin on her face.

"Wayne, don't!"

He whipped around and saw a skeleton and Hildegard rush to his side. The gnome waved her hands at the fairy, and the small creature flew off in a huff.

"Master Wayne, are you safe? You aren't hurt, are you?" Hildegard glared at the trees around them. "You didn't give her any personal item of yours, did you?"

"No. She wanted some of my hair. I didn't feel good about it as soon as she told me." He shuddered. "I can't wait to get out of here."

"We're so glad we found you."

The skeleton walked over to him, and he stared at her.

"Don't you recognize me?"

"Eleanor? You're the skeleton woman from my dreams?"

"Yes, I am." She stared at the ground. "I wish I could've told you sooner. I didn't want you to find out who I am this way."

"So you're the Ferryman's daughter." He nodded when she stayed quiet. "And you also live in Garland Falls and run a bookstore." He waited for her to explain her situation. "I need to think about this for a few minutes."

"I understand. This is a big secret, and I'm not who

you thought I might be."

"Master Wayne, Mistress Eleanor is still the same woman you met at your friend's party. Like you, she has two sides."

"How does this work?" He lifted her bony hand and caressed it. "I mean, you're flesh and blood in Garland Falls."

"The magical realm turns me into my true self. I can be 'alive' while in the mortal world. The Dark Lands turn me back into my skeleton form."

Wayne walked over to a tree stump and started to sit, then he jumped up to check he didn't sit on a tiny fairy. "We're kind of in the same boat. It turns out while I'm here, I can shapeshift into whatever race is nearby." He stared at Hildegard and felt his body shrink to her size. No nausea, no ill effect, and no bad feelings. "See? Now I'm a gnome. I think I've gotten the hang of this."

"You have a powerful ability." Eleanor walked over to him. "But what about what we have? We've had some special times together. Do you think your leprechaun luck will doom us?"

"I don't think so. Like I said, I need to think about this." He stared at Eleanor, then laughed and startled what sounded like twenty birds in the nearby trees. "Okay, I've thought about it. Eleanor, you're you, and I love both sides of you. I think we can make this work." He stood and took her hands. "We'll be the strangest couple any realm has ever seen. Come on. Let's get to the Light Side and back to Garland Falls where we belong."

"You still want to be with me?"

"Of course. I feel complete when I'm with you. A hollow ache sits in my stomach when we're apart."

"I feel the same way about you."

Hildegard jumped up and down and clapped her hands. "You two are perfect together. Master Lucas was right when he said he could see love around you."

"Remind me to never doubt a Green Man again." Wayne hugged the two women he'd wanted to see most ever since he was taken. "So why did the fairy want my hair? Did she have some diabolical purpose, or is she into some weird stuff?"

"Fairies are rather complicated." Eleanor scanned the area as they traveled. "Sometimes they want an item from mortals so they can have a measure of control over a person. They'll tell the mortal they need gifts for some made-up reason. The real reason is they like to take possessions."

"Are all fairies like this or just the ones here?"

Hildegard patted his hand. "Very few fairy tribes are like this, Master Wayne. The crystaling fairies in the winter kingdom are very kind, and so are many of the others." She glanced around them, as though she expected an army of fairies to fly at them at any moment. "I believe it's because these particular fairies live so close to the Dark Lands. It's in their nature to act the way they do."

Wayne smiled and squeezed Hildegard's hand. "Then I'll have to forgive them for their possessiveness and greed. Maybe one day I'll come back and give them a present."

"A gift would be very generous of you." Eleanor held his other hand. "The fairies here are never shown any kindness. When they are, it's a rare occurrence. I know they'd appreciate any generosity from you."

Wayne took seven gold coins out of his pocket and

laid them on the tree stump. He spied a group of the small fairies in the tree as they watched him lay the coins down. He bowed to them and turned with Eleanor and Hildegard, and they continued down the path.

"I'll start with these. Maybe they can use the coins for something they need."

Eleanor took his hand as the fairies eyed the coins before grabbing them up and flying off. "That was nice of you."

They walked for another hour, Wayne limping more and more. He slowed down and stopped. Eleanor turned to him and motioned for Hildegard to help him.

"I've got to take these boots off for a minute. My feet are raw, and I hate these clothes. How can ogres stand to wear this stuff? I've never missed socks or cotton or polyester so much in my life."

"Ogre skin is much tougher than yours, Master Wayne."

As he eased the boots off, Hildegard gasped.

Eleanor knelt down and gently took his feet in her hands. "You can't go on like this, Wayne. Some of these blisters have opened, and they'll get infected if we don't treat them. Hildegard, did we pack any ointment or water to help heal them?"

The gnome opened the bag, rummaged through it, took out different items, and placed them on the ground. She mumbled to herself about the folly of not being prepared enough when she held up some ointment and gauze in triumph. "I thought Master Wayne might have been hurt when he'd been taken. I didn't pack any water, though." Hildegard handed the items to Eleanor and stood back. "I'm sorry I didn't grab cloth to cover his feet."

Eleanor began to clean the blisters. "The gauze will work for now, but the sooner we get to the Light Side, the better. I wish I had some water to wash these out first, but I'll have to work with what I've got."

"Eleanor." He raised her skull so he could look her in the eye sockets. "You don't have to do this. I can take care of myself. You did enough when you came to find me. You don't have to play nursemaid to me also."

"I care for you, Wayne. As we've said, we have a connection. Taking care of you gives me peace." She finished and eased his boots back on. "Besides, when we return to Garland Falls, I expect a good dinner at Sal's Diner and definitely cookies from Heavenly Bites." She stood, held her hand out, and pulled him to his feet. "And for more help in my store until you go back east."

"I think I can manage what you asked if Hildegard is invited, too."

"Of course." She gazed upward. "We'd best get a move on. The less time we spend out here, the better."

As they started off again, Wayne sighed in relief. His feet didn't sting as badly now. He still couldn't wait to put socks on, though.

Chapter Seventeen

Wayne pointed to the sky, feeling the warmth of the colorful arc fill him. "Can you guys see the rainbow? I thought it would vanish after the sun sets, but it stays up there all the time." He glanced at each of them. "The people in Garland Falls can't see it."

"We saw the rainbow as soon as we started to look for you. The rainbow is how we found you." Eleanor walked a little closer to him. "I'd always heard you found leprechaun treasure at the end of the rainbow. However, I didn't think it would be a mortal man."

"Is it because St. Patrick's Day is so close?"

She shrugged. "The leprechauns are very private and don't help other residents of any realm much. They don't share a lot of their lore with people. We aren't sure if the leprechauns here celebrate St. Patrick's Day."

"I've got something else to show you. Watch this." Wayne held his hand up toward the sky. The rainbow flowed down and spiraled around him. When he raised his hand up, the rainbow flowed into the sky. "Tell me a normal leprechaun has this ability."

The two women looked at each other before Hildegard stepped closer. "I don't know of any leprechaun who has such power to call down light from the sky. I think you are more special than anyone knows."

"The ogres know. Odara told me Chief Argus fears

my power. The brownies also want whatever power they claim I possess. When we get to the Light Side, what will happen to me there? Do you think they'll also want to keep me because of this power?"

Eleanor shrugged, and her bones cracked as they moved against each other. "I wish I could tell you no, but I don't think they've ever seen anyone like you before."

He grinned and held her skeletal hand in his. "I guess we'll find out. I wish I had my return key. If any situation got too bad, we could leave anytime we wanted."

She reached into her pocket and pulled out the large, brass key. "You mean this return key? Hildegard brought it to me when she discovered you were taken."

"I could kiss both of you."

"Not me, Master Wayne." The gnome winked at him. "But I'm sure Mistress Eleanor wouldn't mind a kiss from you."

His smiled grew wider as he gazed at Eleanor. "Is this true? You wouldn't mind a kiss from me?"

"You did kiss me when we were in Garland Falls, you know. I believe this would be our second kiss, if you want to be technical. I mean, if you don't mind a kiss from someone with no lips."

"I do want to kiss you. I like you no matter what you look like. I think I might more than just like you."

He leaned close as she turned her head up. He gently touched his lips to where hers would be if she were flesh and blood. Her arms wrapped around his waist, and he held her close. He didn't care about her skeleton side. He considered her to be the most beautiful woman, no matter what she looked like. At Hildegard's gasp, they broke apart.

Wayne looked the gnome, who had covered her mouth with her hands. "What's wrong, Hildegard?"

"You've changed, Master Wayne. You look like Mistress Eleanor now."

Wayne stepped back from Eleanor and held his hands up. Sure enough, where once there had been flesh, blood, muscle, and tissue, he now had white bones. He felt his head and nope, no hair, no eyebrows, no lips, and no skin. The change had happened so quickly; Wayne felt maybe he did have a measure of control over it now.

"This is strange. This is a weird sensation to not be able to feel my heartbeat." He grabbed his pants when they slipped off his bony hips. "I know I'm alive, but I don't feel part of the living world. It's kind of cool."

"It took me some time to get used to it also. My dad laughed at me while I adjusted between skeleton and flesh."

"You know, this shapeshift power has made our relationship a hundred times easier. In Garland Falls, we can be flesh and blood. Here, I can be a skeleton like you and blend in better with the natives."

She laced her fingers through his and laid her head briefly on his shoulder. "I was so worried you wouldn't want me when you saw my true form."

"And now?"

"Now I'm not worried at all. I believe we are meant for each other."

As they continued down the winding path, Wayne concentrated and turned back to himself. He thought about what he could do and how much easier it had gotten the more he shifted. At times, he could feel the change happen, and other times, like now, it took him by surprise. And he'd thought his life couldn't get any stranger.

He put his arm around Eleanor's waist. "You know, a lot of the people in Garland Falls want me to stay."

"You can count me as one of those people if you like."

He held her hand as they exited the woods onto a better kept path. "Lucas Callahan said you and I would be good together. He also said a lot of people could use my accounting skills. While I walked on Main Street the other day, a store came up for rent. Then he told me a house will be for sale when his assistant gets back from his honeymoon."

"It sounds like the town wants you to stay, as well as the people." She tightened her hold on his hand. "What do you want to do? This is your decision because it's your life. Don't think about what I said when I told you I wanted you to stay."

"I'm happy to know you want me there. I like Garland Falls, but I have a great job back east. However, I think a lot of my co-workers would like to see me gone. If I left, my partnership position would open up. I worked so hard to get where I'm at in my company." He smiled at her and pulled her closer. "But New Jersey doesn't have you."

"That's kind of you to say." She walked quietly for several minutes. "You sound like you've made up your mind."

"I think I have. If you, the people, and the town want me there, I'd be a fool to not listen."

The sky had turned darker as the sun began to set.

"Mistress, we must find somewhere to stop for the night. It wouldn't do to walk into the Light Side without a decent night's rest. We must be prepared for whatever might happen."

"I believe we're near the home of one of my dad's friends. We should be able to find shelter there." She turned to Wayne. "We can also go back to Garland Falls right now if you want. We have the return key. We don't need to get to the Light Side any longer."

"I'm tempted, but I want to meet my mother's family, and this might be my best chance. I have to know why they didn't help her and my father when they needed it the most."

"Of course. I understand." She laid her hand on his arm. "Let's get to some shelter. We can return home whenever we want."

They started down a side trail Eleanor told them would take them to a place where they could rest. A large but tidy cabin stood in the center of a clearing with a fountain off to the left side. Flowers circled the foundation, and smoke drifted up from the stone chimney. The well-maintained yard didn't have a weed or dirt patch anywhere he could see. Birds sang all around them, and Wayne swore he saw a deer beyond the trees. Whoever lived here had high standards and a fondness for nature.

They stepped onto the porch, and the front door flew open. A large bear of a man laughed and lifted Eleanor off her feet. He stood close to seven feet tall with long, tawny hair held back by a leather cord. A large, bushy beard, the same color as his hair, flowed down to his chest in a thick wave. He wore a green flannel shirt tucked into blue jeans. His work boots were covered with dirt and dried mud, and his green eyes sparkled with laughter.

"Eleanor, my girl, it has been too long since your

last visit. How are you? How are your parents?"

"Everyone is fine, Finn." She stepped back when he put her down. "These are my friends Wayne and Hildegard. Can we trespass on your hospitality for the night?"

"Of course." He stepped to the side and waved them in. "Why have you traveled so far out this way? You're closer to the Dark Lands than you should be with two Light Siders as your traveling companions. Rumors have circulated the ogres search for someone important. This someone is said to be quite powerful and belongs to their tribe."

"I guess you could say it's me, sir."

Wayne stood tall, but Finn towered over him.

"The ogres kidnapped me from Garland Falls. I had it out with Chief Argus, and he locked me up. After I got out, the brownies ambushed me. To tell you the truth, I don't want to be anyone's prisoner anymore."

Finn's boisterous laugh rattled the walls and shook the floor. "I can imagine how bothersome it could be. You are welcome here without fear of harm to you. What is this power they all claim you have?"

"I can shapeshift, see a rainbow no one else can, and gold coins fill my pockets by themselves." Wayne shrugged as he stared at Finn. "I didn't even know I had power until the ogres dragged me to the Dark Lands. I think when they brought me here, the magic I carry woke up inside of me."

Finn walked them to the living room and gestured for them to sit. "Then I suppose it's a good thing you made it to the Light Side before they got any closer. Have you all eaten?"

"No, Master Finn, we haven't." Hildegard

rummaged in the bag Eleanor had dropped at her feet. "Our supplies have gotten low. I've tried to be conservative, and Mistress Eleanor doesn't need to eat."

Finn nodded and walked toward the kitchen. "Rest yourselves. I'll make us some dinner, and then you can tell me the rest of your story."

Wayne took in the rustic décor of the cabin. No animal heads and the carved wooden furniture had a high shine. A light-brown area rug covered most of the floor. Its softness spoke of its animal owner, but Finn didn't strike him as someone who would kill any creature for its fur. A large stone fireplace took up most of the far wall, the iron tools off to one side. A long couch and several chairs with tables between them completed the room. Even though the room had a sparse décor, it had a comfortable, almost familiar feel.

Wayne stared in the direction Finn had left in. "Are you sure we can trust him? I'm expecting my bad luck to make itself known anytime now. You have to admit, a lot hasn't gone my way here or in the mortal world."

"You can trust him." Eleanor leaned closer. "He's Lucas and Parker's uncle. He's another Green Man. He'd rather stay here at his home than go to Garland Falls. He looks after the animals in the forest and cares for the flora."

"Well, it would explain why his yard looks so nice." He glanced again toward the kitchen and waiting for Finn to reappear at any second. "He looks a lot like his nephews. Does he ever go see the Callahan brothers?"

She chuckled. "Of course. He went back for both of their weddings. When either couple has a baby, he'll go back for that and any other special event. He loves his family, but he stays here to make sure no Dark Lander or

Light Sider gets out of hand. He's got the ear of the Green Prince, and no one wants him to call *that guy* in. The prince gets testy when he's bothered too much."

"So you say I can trust any of the Green Men we might meet." He looked at her and smiled when she nodded. "It's nice to know there's someone we can trust in this crazy world."

Finn brought in three bowls of stew and set them down. The aromatic steam from them made their stomachs growl.

As soon as he appeared with the food, Wayne inhaled the delicious scent of meat, vegetables, and spices. He dipped his spoon into the thick meaty broth and blew on the steam. "I hope we haven't taken your dinner from you."

"Not at all. I always make extra so I don't have to think about what to have the next night. Don't say another word until you've all eaten and relaxed for a bit."

Wayne ate in silence, finally able to relax without fear of being attacked. Eleanor's status as the Ferryman's daughter had made their travels easier. The ogres and the brownies had no desire to incur the wrath of the one person who ferried their souls to the afterlife.

And to think, she'd fallen for him. He smiled at her and wished he could see her smile and not her skeletal grin. He missed seeing the sparkle in her eyes when she smiled or talked about books or did anything that made her happy. He'd fallen hard for her, too, and faster than he'd believed possible. Who would have thought a skeleton could be so beautiful or that a half ogre, half leprechaun would be lucky enough to find her?

Chapter Eighteen

Finn cleaned up their bowls when they finished and settled back in his chair. He lit a pipe and crossed his legs at the ankles. He tapped the pipe bowl with one enormous finger as he glanced at the three of them. "Relate to me again how you came to be here."

Wayne went through how he'd been kidnapped one more time and how he'd ended up in the ogre tribe. Finn smiled when Wayne told him how he had spoken to the chief and refused to stay in the village. His voice softened when he spoke about Odara, the healer ogre, and how she'd helped him. First, she'd taken care of his aches and pains, then had given him clothes when she helped him escape. Then he talked about the whole business with the brownies.

Finn puffed on his pipe for a few minutes when Wayne finished his tale. He set it off to the side in a small, ceramic tray on the table next to him. "I would very much like to meet Odara. She sounds like she has the most sense of anyone in the village."

"She became a good friend to me. She told me she and my father were friends before he and his family were banished." Wayne's hand curled into a fist when he remembered how the chief had tried to excuse himself from the blame. "I could forgive the betrayal if any of his family had tried to help him when the Huntsman showed his hand."

Finn stroked his beard. "Ah yes. The Huntsman and his hounds have hunted both Light Side and Dark Lands for spirits to take into servitude. I felt my nephew's power stop him before he could take any others that Halloween night."

He chuckled and continued to stroke his beard. "The Huntsman railed about his failure for almost a full year. He can't return to Garland Falls to take revenge, either. The elders have learned their lesson about how to keep the wards and runes around the town maintained. Took them long enough and I bet Adelaide Hall rode them about it the whole time."

Wayne grinned. "I've heard rumors to that effect." He glanced at the floor before he returned his gaze to Finn. "Parker and his wife fought the Huntsman to a standstill and freed those he'd already captured."

Finn leaned forward in his chair. "Don't sell yourself short, Wayne. I sensed the power in you. Your ogre strength helped keep you in the land of the living. Oh, Parker anchored you, but you stepped into the fray with no knowledge of the fight you'd gotten yourself into."

"He hunted my father for most of his life." Wayne stared at the Green Man. "I couldn't let him terrorize either of my parents any longer. My friend Renee told me my love for them helped boost the strength I had to fight him off."

"Love is one of the most powerful emotions anyone can carry with them." He stood and gestured for the others to do the same.

They followed him outside to the back of his house.

"All these rose bushes exploded into the largest blooms I'd ever seen after your fight. They haven't returned to their normal size either. I think they intend to remain this way for a long time."

Wayne walked closer to the nearest one as the fragrance reached him while he stood at least ten steps away. The roses weren't just red. They were brilliant and fiery, with petals the size of his thumbs. He looked back at Finn, who smiled and nodded. Wayne touched a finger to a petal, and the velvety softness surprised him. The petal felt more like a thick, fleece throw blanket than a flower.

As he walked down the row of rose bushes, the fragrance made him light-headed and joy filled him until he thought he'd explode. He reached out again, and the rainbow light shot down from the sky to circle him and flow around the garden. The flowers absorbed the light, and they glowed bright and almost danced from the force of the colorful light.

"How is this possible?" Finn stood next to Wayne, and the rainbow surrounded him also. "I've never heard of anyone with the power to call the light from the sky."

Wayne raised his hands back up, and the rainbow returned to its rightful place. When it returned to the sky, the light looked twice as bright as before. "I think this is the power everyone I meet wants to control. I don't know how they can know how it works if even I don't know."

The trees and bushes rustled with the sound of a large creature or animal. Their stares shot to the forest, and Hildegard pressed closer to Wayne's legs as they all stood in a loose circle. Some sort of large beast snarled, and heavy footsteps sounded closer than they had any right to be. They backed toward the cabin, their gazes still on the trees around them.

"Come, children, let's get back inside. Even though

you're out of the Dark Lands, there's still no reason to not be cautious." Finn stared at the woods. "Dark Landers will follow you no matter how far you travel from their territory. Best not to give them any more temptation to try and make mischief."

They hurried back inside, and Finn bolted the door shut.

"Come here, Wayne." When he walked over, Finn took his hands and stared into his eyes. "Yes, you do carry a powerful magic. Now since I've seen what you can do, I can understand why so many tribes are after you."

"You know, when I found out Renee had magic in her, I got jealous. I worked hard to get where I wanted to be in my work, and all the time she had this special power." He stared at his hands. "Now I have my own abilities, so I don't think I'm quite so jealous any longer. Magic is more work and a lot more trouble than people realize."

Finn let out his loud, boisterous laugh again, and they all smiled.

"You have spoken the truth, my boy. It's not at all what people think it is, but you have a real gift."

"I noticed it a little after I fought the Huntsman. I think he jump-started whatever I can do. I catch glimpses of fairies and movement out of the corner of my eye all the time." He paced in front of the large fireplace. "When I got Renee and Parker's invitation to their party, I noticed how it all escalated then. I would catch the rainbow following me, and it flowed through the invitation. The leprechaun gold showed up in my pockets soon after."

Eleanor spoke up. "I had started to talk to Wayne in

his dreams. Mom had seen the importance of his presence in Garland Falls. So I told him but couldn't tell him why. I knew he needed to be there, and I did feel like he could use some protection. I didn't think the ogres would break into Dee Warner's bed-and-breakfast and take him by force, though."

Finn stroked his beard as he stared into space. "Dee should've sensed when they opened a Dark Lands door. I wonder why she didn't have more protection in place."

"Maybe she knew Master Wayne had to come here."

They all turned to Hildegard, and she gazed at each person in turn.

"Since he's come, he's gotten answers about his father. He's discovered he carries a powerful magic and can pull the rainbow from the sky. When we get to the leprechaun clan, he'll know more about his mother. I think Miss Dee knew he had to come. We all know she has reasons for what she does and says, even if she's the one person who knows what her reason could be."

"Very true. I find Dee Warner to be quite the puzzle, but her charm is undeniable." Finn glanced at his grandfather clock. "Get some rest, children. The sun will rise before you know it, and you still have a fair distance ahead of you."

He passed out blankets and pillows and shuffled to the back of the cabin. Eleanor forced Wayne take the couch while Hildegard made a spot on the floor. Eleanor eased his boots off and checked his feet. They were still red and had a few small blisters, but the angry look around the sores had subsided a little. She doctored him up and left the bandages off for the night and made sure the blanket didn't cover his feet.

Wayne reached out and took her hand. "Thanks

157

again for what you've done for me, Eleanor. I'm glad I met you as a woman and a skeleton. You're beautiful in both forms."

"I wish I wore my flesh form right now so I could blush." She pressed her skull to his forehead. "Get some sleep. I'll re-bandage your feet before we head out tomorrow."

"Good night, Eleanor."

He closed his eyes and thought about the next day. How would the leprechauns react when they met him? Would he be strong enough to demand answers about his mother? He'd done it to the ogres, but some instinct told him he might need to take a different tack with his mother's clan. Leprechauns were reputed to be a tricky race.

****

The next day, Finn filled Eleanor's bag with provisions. They should get to the leprechaun border before midday if they had no more complications. Wayne rolled his eyes. He feared the more likely possibility of things not going their way. If they traveled on actual business, he wouldn't be this worried. However, this time he needed to depend on his very unpredictable personal luck.

Before they left, he paused and turned to Finn. "Do you think my ogre heritage could be the reason I have so many problems in my personal life?"

Again, Finn stroked his beard. "I would say it's possible, but it might be a better question for the leprechauns to answer. I've never heard about the luck of the ogres. This may be a new development. I think your mother's clan is the best place to find out what you need to know."

"I thought so, too. I wanted your opinion before I go to another clan. I'm not sure about what their motives might be."

Finn laid his large hand on Wayne's shoulder. "Trust yourself and your newfound power. If they try any funny business, you'll know what to do. Ogres have good instincts about when they might be attacked. You have those also. Depend on them."

"Thanks, Finn. I'm glad I got to meet you."

The Green Man winked. "You might see me again. You never know what the future holds."

They waved and headed out. Wayne couldn't wait to meet his mother's family, but at the same time, he wished he could be back at Miss Dee's with a plate of her delicious food and, yes, a cinnamon roll.

The sun rose higher in the sky, and Wayne called a halt. "My feet are in a lot of pain. I need a few minutes to rest."

Eleanor pulled his boots off and checked them again. "They have started to heal, and I can't see any signs of infection. I know the soreness is still there, but it should ease over time."

"I hope you're right."

Hildegard patted his leg. "Master Wayne, someone has decided to watch us."

Chapter Nineteen

A full troop of leprechauns jumped out from the bushes and brandished swords and clubs. Hildegard grabbed their bag of provisions and held it tightly to her chest. Wayne glared at them until Eleanor laid her bony hand on his arm and shook her head. The three of them looked at each other before they raised their hands as they stood.

"Who are you?" Wayne narrowed his eyes and wondered why his so-called ogre skills had failed him. Maybe the leprechauns didn't want to attack, at least not yet. "We don't mean you any harm."

A soldier a little taller than the rest stepped forward. "You have trespassed into the land of the leprechauns. You are now our prisoners."

Wayne grinned at Eleanor and Hildegard. "Well, here we go again. I'm so glad I've gotten used to this. I think it's funny now more than bothersome." He stared at the leader of the troop. "Take us to where we need to go. You can put your weapons away. We promise not to cause any problems on the way to wherever."

"The name's Patrick O'Reilly or Captain O'Reilly to you." He stepped forward and poked Wayne with the tip of his sword. "And my troops will sheath their swords when I say and not because you told them to."

"Whatever you say, Captain. We're the epitome of cooperation."

The leprechaun troop surrounded the trio and led them down a different path than the one they'd planned to take. Patrick continued to poke Wayne with his sword while they passed through the changing landscape. When he'd gotten the brief glimpse before, Wayne knew the Light Side would be beautiful.

Trees with bright-green leaves shielded the path from the bright-yellow sun overhead. Flowers of every color waved their full blooms as they passed. He'd never seen so many varieties of butterflies in his life. No debris hindered them, and they had an easier time on the clearer trail. Did he still reside in the Light Side lands, or had he gone into a princess animated movie? He expected the foliage to break into song like cartoon characters at any moment.

He prayed the leprechaun troop would take him to where he wanted to go. He wanted answers, nothing else. They wouldn't deny him such a simple request, would they? With how many times he'd been grabbed, he'd begun to doubt he would ever get any answers. And if Patrick didn't stop with the pokes every few seconds, he'd show the leprechaun captain his own leprechaun temper.

They arrived on the outskirts of a small village. Time to find out what surprises were in store for them as they arrived. They were marched into the middle of a clearing surrounded by small houses. Other leprechauns came to stare at them and whisper among themselves. The leprechauns separated Wayne out and forced him away from Eleanor and Hildegard. He dug his heels in and refused to budge.

"Wait," he said. "My companions come with me, or we leave right now."

Patrick poked Wayne's leg with his sword. "Our king wants a word with you in private. Your friends will be safe until we're told what to do with them."

Wayne snatched the sword out of the leprechaun's hand. "Poke me with this sword one more time, and you and I will have a real problem. I'll hang on to this until we get to our destination. Now, let's go see your king."

Patrick huffed and sputtered but led the way through the woods to a palace built into and around a tall tree. Wayne handed the sword back when Patrick pointed to the king's home.

Wayne took a deep breath and pushed open the door. He ducked his head as he entered. "I'm going to end up a hunchback with how many tiny homes I've been in."

He gazed around in wonder as he stepped farther in and straightened up. The king's throne room rose to a height of at least twenty feet or more, and he gave silent thanks he wouldn't add another ache to his already sore body.

The king's home met his expectations of what a leprechaun palace should be. Fur pelts covered the floor, and bright tapestries hung on the walls. Portraits of kings past hung in between the tapestries, some serious, others jovial. Wayne inhaled the wood scent of the throne room. The whole aroma took him back to the times he and his father had gone to the lumberyard. *Must be handy to have your palace built into a large tree.*

Wayne walked up to where the king sat on his throne and bowed. "I'm honored to meet you, sire. However, I consider it an insult to be treated as a prisoner when my friends and I came here in peace."

At first when the king rose, he stood three feet high. But then his height grew until he could look Wayne in the eye. He wore a simple gold crown on his red hair. A small beard grew on his cheeks and chin, but he had no mustache. He wore an orange-and-white suit with a green velvet cape over his shoulders. Black boots came up to his knees. Rings decorated two fingers on each hand.

"I am King Cullin. Rumors have flown through all the realms a mortal had arrived and caused all kinds of havoc. You've been seen in the Dark Lands." He narrowed his eyes as he glared at Wayne. "Rumors also state you carry a powerful magic within you and want to take over everywhere."

Wayne laughed out loud, and the king stumbled back.

"Those rumors are ridiculous. They're rumors, nothing more. Creatures saw me in the Dark Lands because the ogres kidnapped me. I don't want to be here any more than you want me here. And as for a hostile takeover here? I have to call this rumor the biggest joke of all. I want to go home to Garland Falls."

Cullin stared at him, then nodded. "There is a truth to your words. Tell me your name, sir."

Wayne took a deep breath. What would Cullin say when he heard his last name? His mother might be from this colony. Would he be welcomed or executed in some bizarre way? Did leprechauns execute people? One way to find out so he decided to jump in with both feet.

"My name is Wayne Billings. My mother came from a leprechaun clan, maybe even this one. My father was an ogre from the Dark Lands."

"Yes. Your mother claimed kinship here." The king fell onto his throne, and his chest heaved. "I see her in your eyes and the shape of your face. News had come to us Lily's child didn't survive the Huntsman's attack. How is it you're here?"

Wayne stepped closer and smiled. "My dad saved me. He tried to save my mother, but he couldn't. He ran and took me with him. I've lived in the mortal world all my life. I learned of my heritage and my parents' fate a little over a year ago. My powers kicked in when I arrived in the Dark Lands."

The king covered his eyes and wept silent tears. "My poor sister," he murmured. "I knew she'd been lost, but I had no knowledge of the fate of her love or her child."

"Hang on a second." Wayne stepped closer to the throne. "Did you say you're my uncle?"

Cullin wiped his eyes and smiled for the first time. "I believe I am." He walked to Wayne and grabbed him in a fierce hug. "The whole colony will be glad to see you returned to us."

Wayne pushed out of Cullin's embrace. "Why didn't you help when she needed it? The ogres, I can understand, but you? Aren't leprechauns big on family and clans and stuff?"

"Your mother left here before I took over. Since she married outside our clan, the king at the time got into a bit of a snit she chose an ogre over him." He folded his hands behind his back and started to pace. "He refused to give your parents any refuge or aid when they needed it most. I searched for your family when I took over and hoped to have you all here. I wanted to keep you safe." Cullin hung his head and shook it. "But I was too late to help any of you. Your parents were gone, and you couldn't be found. Now since you are here with us, we shall have a celebration to welcome you into the fold."

"I'm sorry, but I'm not staying here. My home is in

the mortal world, and that's where I belong. I appreciate you wanted to help them, but I came to get answers about my mother. You've given me the information I wanted about her. I do have other questions. Like, can you tell me more about my leprechaun powers?" He held his hands up and stared at them. "I need to know what I can do and why everyone claims to want me to use it for their own purposes."

"I'm not surprised you don't want to stay." Cullin walked to the window on his left while Wayne waited by the throne. "Tell me what has happened with you. You say everyone wants your power?"

"More like they want me." Wayne joined Cullin at the window. "The ogres want to control me. I think the brownies wanted to eat me. Either way, I'm not fond of what people here have in store for me."

"Brownies don't eat people." Cullin turned to him and winked. "They like to make prisoners think they will, but they won't. They have to pretend in order to protect themselves. They're harmless, but the ogres are a different story. I'm glad you got away from them. They would have held you captive for the rest of your life."

"Their healer helped me escape. I'm grateful to her."

"Then she has my thanks also."

"I'm glad to hear you say so. Odara is the one who stood by me in the village." Wayne straightened his shoulders. "However, let me show what I can do. I can shapeshift." At Cullin's raised eyebrow, he concentrated, and his form shrank until he had the size and appearance of the leprechauns outside.

"Your mother had this ability from her birth clan. As she was my sister, I also have this ability. Our whole lineage can shapeshift. It's not rare among leprechauns, but it's not as common as one would think."

Wayne concentrated and shifted back to his regular self. "Come outside. I think what I'm about to show you next will explain why so many people are after me here."

As they stepped outside, the leprechauns all backed away. Wayne walked down to the center of the courtyard, Cullin right behind him. He looked up at the sky and raised his hand. Again, the rainbow flowed down and swirled around him like a colorful robe. Audible gasps reached him, and he smiled at the crowd before he sent the rainbow back to the sky.

"This does explain so much about you." Cullin eyed him with new respect. "As cliché as I know this will sound, there is a prophecy."

"I'd be more surprised if you didn't have a prophecy. What does it say?"

"Someday, a man will come who can call the color from the sky. This man will bring peace to the leprechaun lands. It's very possible you are who we've waited for to help us solve our internal problems." He gripped Wayne's shoulders. "You are indeed a very special leprechaun."

"Are you sure? My leprechaun luck is unpredictable in personal situations. It helps with my business deals, but it becomes iffy in other circumstances. My love life has taken a major hit because of my bad personal luck." He glanced at Eleanor and smiled. "That is, until recently."

Cullin rubbed his chin. "All leprechaun luck is supposed to be good, except to those who abuse it. Love is at the heart of our good luck."

"Maybe my ogre lineage has messed it up."

"It's possible. Another reason could be because your

parents eloped. Your mother never received the blessing from the king." He nodded toward where Eleanor and Hildegard stood. "The skeleton woman and gnome you came in with, who are they?"

Wayne gazed at his friends. Well, one friend and a woman who meant more to him than he could describe. "Hildegard is a friend and companion. Eleanor, the skeleton, is the Ferryman's daughter."

"And she has stayed by you through all your trials." He stared at Wayne, and a small smile curled one side of his mouth. "You have strong emotions for Eleanor?"

Wayne thought about her kindness and sense of humor. How she loved to talk to her customers at her bookstore. How she closed her store to come to the Dark Lands to find him. She held his heart in her bony and flesh hands.

"Yes, I do. Eleanor is so great and the brightest spot in my life right now."

"Then I believe your sporadic luck will straighten itself out the longer you are with her." He studied Wayne and walked around him. "As for your other abilities, I'm not sure what to say. You may have to go to the one who rules the Light Side lands. She should have the answers you need."

"Does she know about the prophecy here?"

Cullin chuckled. "I believe she has knowledge of every kingdom she rules."

"Okay, I guess she's next on the list of people to talk to." He pointed to Eleanor and Hildegard. "Can you have my friends brought over, please?"

Cullin turned to the captain who had stood at attention the whole time. "Escort Wayne's companions here. They are to leave our lands with no further hinderance."

Captain O'Reilly stepped forward. "But sire, we took them prisoner, fair and square."

"Patrick, you've done a wonderful job to keep them contained until we sorted them out," Cullin said. "But now they are our guests, so let's treat them as such."

Partick frowned but bowed. "As you command, Your Majesty."

Wayne walked over to where Eleanor and Hildegard still stood surrounded by the troops. He took their hands. "Would you like to meet my uncle?"

"Yes, of course," Eleanor said while Hildegard nodded. "It's a surprise to find out your royal heritage."

"I wish I'd known. Not because of what Cullin can give me, but to find out more of my family." He looked around the small colony. "I wonder if Mom ever told Dad she had royal blood."

"I bet she didn't."

Hildegard spoke up. "Your father would have insisted she stay with her clan if he'd been privy to this information. Chief Argus would've told you also, if he'd known."

"You're right, Hildegard." Wayne turned to Eleanor and squeezed her hands. "You know, your family is part of the Dark Lands hierarchy. Since I'm royal, does this mean we can get married if we decide to?"

"I suppose so, if you want to spend your mortal life with a skeleton."

"You forget, dear lady," he said. He concentrated and could sense the change occurring in him. "I can look like you."

"I love your bones," she whispered.

"They still aren't as pretty as yours."

Cullin gave them blessings for safe travels and called over Patrick and his troops. "The palace isn't far from here. You should be there by late afternoon. I wish you all the best. Please come back so we can talk more."

Chapter Twenty

"Captain O'Reilly, you didn't have to escort us to see the ruler of the Light Side." Wayne winked at Eleanor and wished he knew if she smiled at him. "I'm pretty sure we can make the trip on our own."

"King Cullin requested you arrive in a proper fashion." He drew himself up higher. "My troops and I are the best soldiers in our clan. You will look more respectable if we are with you."

"So politics are at the heart of it all. I'm not surprised. Somehow, everything always comes down to politics."

Patrick frowned. "Standard protocol and good manners dictate you meet royalty with an escort if you don't have an appointment. Also, maybe you won't get thrown into the dungeon because you are an ogre."

Hildegard covered her mouth as Wayne frowned, his earlier humor faltering for a moment.

"I'm half ogre. I'm also half leprechaun. Why do people keep forgetting that all the time?"

Eleanor laid her hand on his arm. "I'm sure the captain meant no disrespect, Wayne."

Patrick gave a mighty sniff and stomped ahead while the three friends chuckled.

Wayne nodded toward their guide as his good mood came back. "I guess I have the knack to get under his skin too easily."

"Don't push him too hard, Master Wayne. Like brownies, leprechauns can be unpredictable."

Patrick called a halt and held his hand up. "Hush. Listen."

The troop gathered around Wayne, Eleanor, and Hildegard as branches snapped and underbrush rustled off to their left. Someone or something big headed right for them and closed in fast. The circle tightened before a large ogre jumped out from the trees.

"Why have you entered the Light Side without permission?" Patrick held his sword higher, and the troop fanned out as they took their defensive positions. "Return to the Dark Lands, ogre. You have no business here."

"My business doesn't concern you, leprechaun." The ogre glanced at the troop and wheezed out a deep laugh. "My business is with the ogre with you."

The leprechauns along with Eleanor and Hildegard all moved in front of Wayne.

"You won't take Master Wayne or harm him while we can defend him." Hildegard balled her hands into small fists. "Back away, ogre, before we are forced to hurt you."

With a wide sweep of his giant hand, the ogre knocked all the leprechauns out of the way. He reached over and grabbed Wayne by his shirt. "Chief Argus didn't give you permission to leave, boy. You will return to your tribe and make amends to your chief."

Wayne knocked the ogre's hands away, then reached skyward and called the rainbow. He stumbled back out of the ogre's reach as the ogre covered his eyes and shouted. Wayne took several steps back and moved next to his friends. His arms shook, and he forced his jaw to unclench. The ogre's massive size made no difference. He had power to say no to anyone who tried to hurt him and take him away.

"I won't return to the tribe. Tell Chief Argus if he wants, he can come talk to me like a reasonable ogre or not at all. I won't be pushed around by him and his tribe any longer." He spun the ogre around and kicked him on the seat of his pants. "Now go home."

He hurried over to where Patrick lay and kept an eye on the ogre as he lumbered away. He didn't trust the ogre had come alone. Right now, the leprechauns with him needed his help. He didn't have time to worry about who else might be out there.

"Are you okay? He didn't hit you too hard, did he?"

"I've survived worse than this." The captain stood on shaky legs and rubbed his head while he checked on his troops. "We all appear to be unhurt." He turned to Wayne and eyed him with caution. "We haven't been kind to you, and yet you still checked to make sure my injuries weren't serious."

"I'm not like the ogres. I'm not sure I'm like the leprechauns either." Wayne shrugged. "I guess you'll have to take me as I am."

Patrick stuck his hand out, and Wayne shook it.

"We'd best hurry to the palace. More ogres may have come with the one who engaged us. We'd better not tarry here any longer."

"Good idea. I had the same thought myself."

As they hurried down the path, Wayne wondered why his instincts hadn't warned him about the ogre who stalked them. Maybe it had to do with the ogre not wanting to harm him or his friends. This gave him another question to ask the leader of the Light Side. Not even in Garland Falls, but still unanswered questions continued to pile up. How many more questions were bound to crowd his mind before this whole adventure came to a close? Well, he'd find out soon enough.

Wayne and Hildegard were out of breath by the time they stopped in front of tall, wrought-iron gates. Pink roses twined through the design, and the sweet fragrance surrounded them. Soft music drifted out to them on the slight breeze. Patrick nodded at Wayne before he pushed on the gates to open them slowly and steadily.

He led them to a clearing where several fairies sat around small tables. They drank tea from dainty cups and nibbled on cookies from a small platter in the middle of the table. At the far end stood a gazebo, painted white and covered in blossoms of all different colors and scents. The fairies looked up when they entered, and some frowned before they turned back to their conversations.

Wayne glanced at his companions, took a deep breath, and headed for the woman who sat alone in the gazebo. After the fight with the ogre and the hard travel they'd done, they didn't look very presentable to see royalty. He wished they'd had a moment to clean up first. He tried to brush most of the dust and leaves from his pants and shirt. Maybe the queen would give them a pass since they'd traveled a good distance. Eleanor and Hildegard followed on his heels, and they ignored the disdain from the company at the obvious tea party.

Patrick bowed, then turned to Wayne. "I have done my duty and delivered you to where you need to be. My troops and I need to return to our clan. The ogre from the forest concerns me, and I must let King Cullin know." He bowed to the Light Side ruler as she perched on a white, wicker chair. "Forgive my hasty departure, Queen Shayla, but my clan needs me."

"You are forgiven, Captain O'Reilly. My best wishes to your king and family." She smiled at Wayne as she tapped her cheek. "So you are the mortal who's caused so much havoc in our lands."

"Yes, I guess I am, but not by my own choice." He bowed to Shayla and sensed Eleanor and Hildegard did the same. "My name is Wayne Billings."

Shayla's smile grew wider as she gazed at them. "Rumors have circulated through the fairy lands about you for a long time. How did you come to be here?"

"The ogre tribe kidnapped me and brought me here. I had planned a trip here in the future, but the ogres pushed my plans up a bit."

Shayla rose from her chair and stepped down to the grass to watch him. Her dress flowed around her even though the wind didn't blow. Large, glittery wings spread out from her back and caught the sun's rays to magnify them so they shone around the clearing. Her long, silver hair hung down to the backs of her legs. A thin, gold crown perched atop her head. Golden light trailed in her wake as she walked around him. "You travel with a gnome and the Ferryman's daughter. You're an odd trio, indeed."

Hildegard stepped forward and bowed, though her limbs trembled. "When Master Wayne was taken from Delia Warner's, Mistress Eleanor and I had to come find him."

"Delia Warner is part of this too, is she?" Shayla's laugh blended with the music drifting in on the breeze. "I should have known the little winter pixie would be involved somehow." She walked away from them.

"Come with me, children. We shall go inside and refresh ourselves. I should like to hear all about your adventures and the reason why you come to me."

The three of them looked at each other. Wayne shrugged and started after Shayla as she led the way to a white castle, which glittered in the sunlight. He glanced up at the sky and noticed the rainbow had dimmed a bit. He frowned a little as he stared at it.

"Look up," he whispered to the others. "The rainbow isn't as bright as before. Do you think it's a bad sign?"

Eleanor shook her head. "Let's not jump to any conclusions. It may change with your emotions." She took his hand. "I can feel how nervous you are. You need to stop your tremors. You must be strong to deal with fairy royalty. We need Queen Shayla's help to figure out your powers. We'll wait to hear what she says after we tell her our story."

"Your whole speech right then didn't make me feel better."

The room they entered had glass doors flung open on every wall, and a breeze made the curtains flutter. The scent of roses, lavender, lilac, and other flowers surrounded them. Wayne's nerves didn't settle down. Instead, he shuddered as the aromas drifted over him. He shouldn't be nervous around the queen of the Light Side, should he? He eyed the open windows and wanted to make a run for it as soon as Shayla settled herself on what could be described as her throne.

She smoothed out her gown and glanced at each of them in turn. Her gaze stayed on Wayne the longest. "Now, please explain why the ogre chief had you kidnapped."

"He says I have power. I think he wants to use it for himself."

She smiled as she rested her chin on her hand. "You have stated a very grievous charge. Chief Argus is protective of his people. Does he see you as threat?"

"I don't know. I guess it's possible. The former chief cast my father out from the tribe and handed him over to the Huntsman. Maybe he thinks I need to pay the debt the tribe promised." He stepped closer. "However, if you think I would let it happen, think again. I got away from that spectral maniac once. I have no problem fighting him one more time."

Shayla rose, and Wayne swallowed hard. Had he overstepped his bounds? He didn't mean to be disrespectful to the queen. He'd bet she carried more magic in her little finger than he did in his whole body. He stood his ground as she glided toward him. They stared at each other for several minutes. If he concentrated, he knew he'd see the tension in the air hang over them as a dark miasma of doom.

"People in my presence don't take such an aggressive tone with me in my home, Wayne Billings. I allow you this one time, but don't think to speak to me in such a fashion again." Then she laughed as her eyes twinkled with merriment.

He held her gaze for another second before he stared at the floor. "I'm sorry, Queen Shayla. Every time I remember how the ogres treated my father, I lose my temper."

He raised his gaze, and she smiled at him.

"I thought you were angry with me."

"No, I'm not. It's enjoyable to have someone speak their mind and not hide behind pretty words." She walked back to the throne and tugged on a golden cord.

A servant appeared at her side in an instant as her wings beat the air in a furious fashion.

"Please have refreshments brought in for my guests."

Eleanor bowed deep. "You don't have to go to any trouble for us. We don't want to take up a lot of your time."

Shayla waved her words away as she led them to a small room down a side corridor. "I always take tea in here. It's no trouble to accommodate guests. The Light Side always has plenty to spare. And I have another visitor besides you this afternoon." She beckoned to one of her servants who showed Chief Argus in. "The chief came to see me right before you arrived."

Wayne shot to his feet and glared at the ogre chief. "I think we'll leave now, Your Majesty. I knew my instincts said there would be trouble, but I didn't think he'd travel all the way here to grab me."

"Please, Mr. Billings, be calm. Chief Argus is here to plead his case on why you should be returned to the ogre tribe. I agreed to hear him." She picked up a slice of bread and buttered it. "After the little you have told me so far, I find I must agree with you and not the ogres. You should be returned to Garland Falls as soon as you wish to go."

"Thank you, Queen Shayla." He took a sip of his tea. "Between the ogres, the brownies, and the leprechauns, I think I've had enough of the fairy realms."

"The boy can open the door to the Dark Lands whenever he chooses." Argus sat back and folded his arms. "He can't be allowed access anytime he feels the urge to come through."

Wayne leaned forward, and he narrowed his eyes as he glared at the chief. "I didn't want to open that particular door the first time either. You'll have to trust I'll stay on my side of the door. I expect the same of you."

"And what of your power? Answer me, boy." Argus turned to Shayla, and his scowl deepened the crevices on his face as his brow hung low. "He can pull the light from the sky with but a thought."

"Is this true, Wayne?"

He hesitated, afraid of what she'd say. "Yes. I discovered I can summon the light. I didn't know anyone could call the rainbow to them, but apparently, I can."

Shayla sipped her tea and glanced at Wayne. "Your mother had that power." She replaced her cup with a quiet clink. "Of course, she didn't have the strength to wield the light like you do, but she could call the rainbow to her."

"What do you mean 'wield it'? The rainbow can be used as a weapon?"

She dabbed at the corners of her mouth with a lace napkin. "No one knows for sure how the rainbow's light can be used. She married your father and left before anyone realized she'd gone." Her eyes took on a faraway look. "Lily had such a tiny, frail stature, even by leprechaun standards. Her abilities would have grown stronger if she'd stayed to receive the blessings of her king."

"How do you know all this?" Wayne glanced at his companions and had no interest to see the anger on Argus' face. "Did you know her?"

"I made her a member of my court. Many men vied for her hand, but she found the ogre who she wanted to love. She snuck Edmund McGee into my castle here so I could meet him. My surprise at his features made them smile. I didn't think some ogres could pass for human. I found him to be quite handsome for an ogre. I've never seen such love and devotion in two people. They were a perfect match."

Wayne smiled. "I could tell by the way my father talked about her and their marriage how much he loved her. My father never got over her death, and he did what he could to protect me." He closed his eyes and opened them when Eleanor took his hand. "They didn't deserve to be hunted and tormented for the rest of their lives." He glared at Argus. "I blame you for what they suffered."

"There are more than me to carry blame, boy." Argus stood and leaned on the table. "Ask the leprechauns why they also didn't give aid to your parents."

"I did. Turns out the former king carried a lot of jealousy toward my parents. So I won't give allegiance to you or the leprechauns." He stood and pushed his chair back. "You made this trip for no reason, Argus. Go back to your tribe. I won't ever come back to you."

"A grudge is serious to hold on to, boy." Argus stepped closer. "Here in the fairy realms, a grudge can and will take on a life of its own. You need to consider your actions."

Wayne turned his back and walked toward the door before he looked over his shoulder. "So be it. Whatever the consequences, you can carry the blame for those also."

Chapter Twenty-One

Wayne stormed out the room, Eleanor and Hildegard right behind him. He pushed through the tables of fairies, ignoring their stares and mumbled comments. He stopped at the gates and leaned his head against the cool metal. His heart pounded in his chest, his blood rushing through his veins. A roar in his ears muffled the approach of his friends. He glanced at Eleanor when she laid her skeletal hand on his shoulder.

He dropped his head as his shoulders drooped with the release of the tension he'd held on to. "Sorry, but if I stayed in there one more minute, I would have said something awful or done a regrettable action."

"We understand." Eleanor held up the return key. "Chief Argus made a good point, you know. If you hold on to a grudge long enough, it can take on a life of its own. The fairy realms are different from the mortal world. All you do or say has consequences, either good or bad. Try and find some forgiveness for the ogre tribe, or we can go home now if you want."

"I wish we could leave, because I really don't want to stay in this realm any longer than we have to." He shook his head and turned to lean against the gates. "Maybe we'll go home tomorrow. I need to find out if she knows what else I can do."

"You may get your chance now, Master Wayne." Hildegard pointed toward the castle. "The queen comes this way, Chief Argus behind her."

"Great." He straightened up and stared at the two people who walked his way. "I don't want to talk to Argus right now. He has a tendency to set off my temper."

"Try and be calm." Eleanor held his hand. "Maybe he's come to apologize."

Wayne glanced at her and snorted. "I doubt he'd apologize to me. We don't see eye to eye on this situation."

Shayla stopped before them and gestured to Argus. "Mr. Billings, I have asked the chief to return to his home. You and I will discuss this situation in more detail. Then I will determine without a doubt where you belong."

"Now wait a minute…"

Eleanor squeezed his hand and shook her head. "Be careful how you answer."

Wayne glared at the pair in front of him. "Fine, but I will return to Garland Falls, with or without your permission."

"If all of you will leave us, we should be able to get this matter settled to everyone's satisfaction." She clapped her hands, and several fairies appeared and bowed low. "Please take Eleanor and Hildegard somewhere they can rest."

Wayne watched as his friends were led away as Argus stomped through the gates. "It's you and me now, Your Majesty. How do you think we can resolve this whole mess?"

She walked toward a walled-in garden, leaving him no choice but to follow. Once inside, she sat on a stone bench and gestured for him to take a seat next to her. "As

I see it, neither the ogres nor the leprechauns can claim you as their own. Your life is in the mortal world."

"Agreed."

"However, Chief Argus and I must agree on one particular point." She stared at the sky and pointed to the rainbow. "You have to let go of the grudge you carry. You'll never have full control over what you can do until you let your heart forgive. Once you do, your soul and your powers will heal."

"I understand, but this is a hard thing you ask." He reached out and touched a rose, and the flower glowed bright for a few seconds before it returned to normal. "My mother died not long after she had me. I never had a chance to know her. My father kept us moving around for most of my life." He shook his head and folded his hands. "All because of some petty jealousies from two tribes. I find it hard to forgive the ogre tribe or the leprechaun clan."

"Times were so different back then. The leaders of both ogre and leprechaun held tight to the old ways and laws. They didn't mean to be cruel. They had never encountered a situation like your parents."

"I hope times have changed here. People's lives would be so much easier if they have."

"I believe all the realms here have become more tolerant in recent years."

Wayne stared at her. "You knew my parents. Why didn't you step in to help or at least offer them a safe place to stay?"

Her wings twitched, and she frowned a little. "As in the mortal world, politics do rule here in the fairy realms as well. My hands were tied by the fairy laws at the time. I have since disbanded those centuries-old rules." She smiled at him. "Trust me when I say the fairy lands, both light and dark, are much better than they used to be. But you must learn how to forgive."

"What if I can't?"

Shayla stood and walked a few steps away, then turned. "Then your leprechaun luck will always doom you to be alone. Your anger and the grudge you carry will ripple through all the fairy realms, and there will be consequences. You must forgive and ask for the blessing of the leprechauns and the ogres. If you can do this one simple act, your powers will blossom and grow."

"You make it sound so easy. Forgiveness is harder to do than anyone thinks."

"You have to believe in the simplicity of the act. Yes, forgiving someone is hard, but when you think about it long enough, it's actually very easy."

"I guess I have to try. I mean, if you have that much faith in me." He stood and glanced around at the walled garden and all the flowers contained within. "So after I forgive everyone who hurt me, I'll have more control over when I shapeshift and the rainbow?" He reached into his pocket and pulled out three gold coins. "Will these coins continue to appear? What about Eleanor? Could we have a future together?"

"I don't know if the coins will always fill your pockets." She closed his fist around them and laid her hands on his. "Remember, all of your other questions will be answered in time with love and forgiveness."

"You make it sound so easy, Your Majesty." He stared at his hands. "Do you think I have the capacity to accomplish this? Can I forgive both sides of my heritage?"

"You have a good heart, Wayne. To forgive such

grievous hurts is within you." She lifted his chin and smiled at him. "You carry the strength for forgiveness and love in you from your parents. Look inside yourself, and you'll find it."

She started to walk away when he stopped her.

"And what about the pot of gold at the end of the rainbow? Will I find it, do you think?"

She winked at him before she gazed at her castle. She walked to the garden's entrance. "Mr. Billings, Wayne, I believe you already have your pot of gold."

He sat on the bench again when the queen left and thought about what she'd told him. His heart knew she had to be right, but to forgive such a heinous betrayal? Could he forgive Argus for his past actions, no matter what the reason? He'd held on to the anger for the past eighteen months, feeding it to let it fester and grow. Maybe he needed to let the anger and hurt go. To carry around such heavy emotions could be the reason his personal life had been in shambles.

He grinned as he considered his father's side of his heritage. He liked his half-ogre side. He'd not been taken advantage of for as long as he could remember. He might have drawn on the ogre part of his parentage to make the bigger, more aggressive people back off. His leprechaun side had certainly given him an advantage when it came to money.

But the heart and not the mind ruled emotions. He needed to clear his heart of the anger and, yes, this ridiculous grudge. He wouldn't hurt anyone but himself if he continued to hold on to these negative emotions. He needed to talk to Cullin and then Argus, to tell them how he felt, and he'd have to keep his temper in check. He marched toward Shayla's castle and winced. Maybe he should ask for some socks first.

He ignored the fairies as they strolled past him when he walked inside. He heard voices and headed toward them. He found Eleanor and Hildegard in conversation with Shayla in the room where they'd had tea earlier.

"I've thought about what you said, Your Majesty. You're right. I can't carry this weight inside me any longer. I'd like your permission to leave and to meet with King Cullin and Chief Argus. If we talk more, without shouts and insults, I might be able to forgive them."

"I'm glad to hear it." She clapped her hands, and two fairies flew in. "Please gather provisions for our guests. They will travel tomorrow."

"Can I ask for another favor?" Wayne pointed to his feet. "Is there any way I can get a pair of socks and maybe a pair of boots in my size?"

Shayla laughed and nodded. "Of course. It's no wonder you've been mistaken for an ogre no matter where you've gone. You're dressed in their garb. I'll have fresh clothes for you before you leave. You should look and feel more like yourself then."

His shoulders sagged as he dropped into the chair next to Eleanor. "My feet and the rest of my body thank you."

Chapter Twenty-Two

The next day, Queen Shayla walked her guests to the gate as the sun rose. She handed the bag of provisions out, and Wayne grabbed it before Eleanor had a chance to take it.

"I want to thank you again for your hospitality and your good advice, Your Majesty," he said. "And let me add a thanks for the new clothes. They fit better than what I wore when I got here."

"You are most welcome, Wayne. I have provided an ointment for the blisters on your feet. I've also given Eleanor fresh gauze and extra bandages if you should need them. I expect your feet to heal much faster now."

He bowed deeply, and Eleanor and Hildegard did the same.

"I'm sorry about how I acted when we first arrived. I never should have spoken to you in such a manner."

"All is forgiven, Wayne." The queen glanced over her shoulder. "I enjoyed all of our conversations. I believe my court and myself have grown complacent over the centuries." She took his hand. "I do hope you'll come back and tell me of your life in the mortal world. I'm curious to know how your situation will work out."

"Since I can open doors to the realms here, you can count on my return. I hope to have full control over this particular power as soon as possible."

She patted the back of his hand. "I'm sure you will.

Remember to forgive those who have wronged your family, and all will fall into place. Oh, and when you get back to Garland Falls, give my regards to Delia Warner. It's been far too long since we've had time to chat."

"I'll give her your message." Wayne eyed the sky and nodded when the rainbow had grown a little brighter. "We'd better get a move on. Thank you again for all you've done."

They waved as they left Queen Shayla's courtyard. The path opened up before them as they set off at a quick pace.

"So what did the queen want to talk to you about yesterday?"

He glanced at Eleanor and smiled when she sounded a bit jealous. "She told me I had to put a lid on my hardheadedness and see situations as they used to be here in the fairy realms. Times have changed since my parents left. She said I need to learn how to forgive."

"And for that she needed to talk to you in private?"

"Who knows why royalty do what they do? She did tell me one more piece of news, though." When Eleanor turned her sightless gaze to him, he smiled even wider. "She implied you might be the pot of gold at the end of my rainbow."

"Oh, Master Wayne, I hope so." Hildegard clapped her hands and scampered in front of them. "Mistress Eleanor will be wonderful for you."

"We'll have to see how my dad feels about this."

Wayne shouldered the bag a little higher. "Hey, I'll even go old school and ask his permission if you want."

"Let's settle all the other problems first. We can talk about this more when we return to Garland Falls." She leaned close and lowered her voice. "However, I think he'll be fine with whatever we want to tell him."

"How can you be so sure?"

She laced her bony fingers through his flesh-and-blood ones. "He wants me to be happy, no matter what choices I make. Of course, if I make a wrong choice, he's always the first to let me know."

Wayne chuckled and held her hand a little tighter. "I'll make sure to tell him I'm a good choice."

By midday, they'd returned to the leprechaun village. Captain Patrick O'Reilly met them at the border and saluted them. "We found no trace of any ogres in our territory. Enter and be welcome, Wayne Billings and companions."

"Thank you, Captain. This is a different welcome from the last one you gave us."

Patrick laughed. "This time, you are attired as you should be and not as an ogre." He waved them forward. "King Cullin has expected you today. Queen Shayla sent word by the dryads you decided to see us again."

Wayne, Eleanor, and Hildegard were taken to the king's tree palace. When the trio stepped inside, Cullin increased his height to greet his visitors in a more proper fashion. "Welcome back, Wayne. I'd hoped you would return."

"I've come to say I thought about what you told me before about my mother. I should have forgiven the clan right away because I knew times were different back then. I also want to ask for your forgiveness for my stubbornness not to believe what you told me."

Cullin grabbed his hands in a firm handshake. "Thank you for your kind words. I appreciate your forthrightness and your forgiveness." He wiped a tear from his eye. "I know how hard it must have been for you to hear how your parents were treated when they fell in love. You know what they say. The heart wants what the heart wants."

Wayne glanced at Eleanor in her skeleton form and smiled. "I can agree with you."

"And as for your stubbornness, it's part of your leprechaun heritage." He leaned close to whisper in a way that couldn't be considered a whisper. "Our race has stubbornness inbred into our very selves."

Wayne laughed and wiped his eye. "I think I've always been aware of my leprechaun stubborn side. It explains a lot in my life."

Cullin led them outside. "You shall stay with us for the rest of the day. I know you have another place to be, so rest here for the night. I would consider it an honorable pleasure."

"Thank you, Cullin. We'll take you up on your generous offer." Wayne looked around and jumped when a small animal scampered out from the forest. "As long as no more ogres show up to kidnap me again."

"My troops will make sure they don't cross into our lands. Tonight, the three of you will stay with me. My palace is the most secure in the whole village."

Wayne and Eleanor walked through the village and talked with the leprechauns. Hildegard stayed with the women and learned different recipes to take back with her to the Ferryman's home. Wayne handed out the gold coins to the children who followed them around.

"Look." Eleanor pointed to the sky. "Your rainbow has grown brighter again."

"Is it weird we can even see it when the sun has started to set?"

"You are in a magical land, don't forget. I don't

think whatever happens here can be called weird." She caressed his cheek before dropping her touch to his chest. "You and the rainbow are connected by your heart. Your rainbow will always be around even if you're the only one who sees it."

He shrugged. "You make a good point." He stared at the rainbow and smiled a little. "I think it's brighter because I know I have to let go of this anger inside me. I've already taken the first steps. The hard part will be to talk to the ogres."

"I'll be with you the whole time."

He put his arm around her bony shoulders. "I know, and trust me when I say I'm grateful for your presence. Hildegard, too. I didn't think I'd want someone to wait on me all the time, but she's a real treasure."

"When we get back to Garland Falls, she'll have to return to my dad's house. It's where she works after all."

Wayne watched the gnome laugh and talk with the leprechauns. "I know, but I'll miss her. I hope she can take time to come back for the occasional visit."

"I don't think you could keep her away."

They continued to wander until the sun set and Cullin called for them to return to his home.

"I fear just because we can't find any sign of the ogres doesn't mean we should take chances. Come inside, and we'll have a nice supper."

The leprechauns brought out stew in brown bread bowls and laid fruit and cheese on the table.

Wayne leaned close to Eleanor who had declined a plate. "Isn't this the part in a movie where situations go wrong in horrible and terrible ways?"

"King Cullin is one of the more honorable leaders in the fairy realms. I don't think he has any nefarious plans for us."

He picked up his spoon and dipped it into the stew. "Good, because I think my stomach has started to consume itself, and I'm wiped out. I haven't walked this much in ages."

"Tomorrow, my troops will escort you to the edge of our lands." Cullin lifted his pewter goblet and took several healthy swallows before he set the mug on the table. "They can't be with you all the way to the ogre village, but you shouldn't have any more problems."

"I hope not." Wayne drank some of the beer in his goblet and choked. His eyes watered, and he grabbed his napkin, relieved he hadn't taken a bigger swallow. "Wow, I didn't think they made beer strong enough to strip paint. Anyway, I hope we don't have to contend with the brownies again. I don't trust them after the last time I met up with them."

Cullin eyed his garments again. "I believe you should be safe this time. You wear the clothes of Queen Shayla. She has had her crest emblazoned on the shirt. They should see the emblem and leave you be."

"I hope you're right."

They finished their meal, and Cullin invited them to sit in front of the fireplace with him. Wayne declined any more leprechaun beer. The one swallow he'd had took his breath away. The king regaled them with leprechaun lore and tales from his own childhood.

His eyes misted over when he talked about Lily. "I miss my sister every single day. I always wanted to believe she got to live her life, but I knew it wasn't true." He looked at Wayne. "I hope you'll come back to see me sometimes. I see her spirit in you, and I would like to know you better."

Soon Wayne's eyes drifted closed from the heavy meal and the warmth from the fire. Eleanor took his arm and led him and Hildegard up the stairs to the bedrooms Cullin said they could use. Wayne watched Eleanor stand by the window. With her on guard, he knew there wouldn't be any trouble that night.

****

Eleanor rose from the bed and stretched. Time to wake the others so they could settle their business and get back to Garland Falls. She shook Wayne and Hildegard awake when the sun rose. "The king wants us to have breakfast before we go. If we leave soon enough, we should get to the ogre village before nightfall."

Wayne rubbed his eyes and stretched. He swung his legs over the side of the bed and yanked on his new boots. "Sounds good. I hope we make it. I'm tired of the outdoors life."

"Come, Master Wayne. It hasn't been so bad."

"I guess it hasn't. Let's go see Cullin before we hit the road. I think I like him better than Argus. He's not nearly as hardheaded."

Eleanor gave him a quick hug. "Give the ogre chief a chance. You may find him more pleasant than you believe him to be."

They headed downstairs to the throne room. Wayne wasn't surprised to see a small contingent of ogres waiting for them there.

Wayne rolled his eyes and sighed. "I don't believe this. If you had waited a couple of hours, I would've been back to see Chief Argus."

The largest ogre stepped forward. "King Cullin sent us a message you are to return to the village today."

Wayne shot a glance at Cullin who shrugged. "Why

am I not surprised?"

The ogre laid a hand on his sword hilt. "He stated you worried the brownies might attack you again. Chief Argus has sent us to escort you back as soon as you are ready to leave."

"Oh." Wayne turned a sheepish smile to Cullin. "Sorry again. I think I've watched too many suspense movies in my life."

"You don't have to apologize, my lad." He gestured to the table. "Now, fill up. Even though you have an escort, that doesn't mean you should dillydally."

Wayne and Hildegard ate while Eleanor checked their provisions. She talked to one of the leprechauns who brought out some of the supplies they were low on. When they all finished, they walked over to the ogre guard.

Cullin stopped them before they left. "Wayne Billings, take with you the blessings and the gratitude of the leprechaun clan. Know you and your companions are welcome here anytime you wish to return."

Wayne took the small pin Cullin handed him. "Thank you, Your Majesty. Your blessing means the world to me. I'll return some time in the future. I'd like to learn more about my family here."

The ogre leader took the bag from Eleanor and slung it over his shoulder. They waved goodbye to the leprechaun clan and started their trek back to the Dark Lands.

Chapter Twenty-Three

Wayne and his friends arrived in the late afternoon. His feet were a lot more comfortable than when he'd been here before. When they arrived, they were taken to Argus. The chief's house didn't have the opulence of the queen's palace or the warmth of Cullin's tree, but the rustic look had a comfortable atmosphere. Wayne grinned. It also fit with the rougher personality of the ogre chief.

"Hello, Chief Argus."

The chief folded his arms and glared at Wayne. "So after all you said at Queen Shayla's castle, you now come back to me. Are you here to stay, like your chief commands?"

"Oh boy. Are you on your same old song again?" Wayne held his hand up. "We've arrived a few minutes ago and don't want to jump into a serious conversation right now. We're tired and would like to freshen up and rest. Can we wait until tomorrow to talk?"

Argus growled deep in his throat. "If you must. The queen has ordered me to listen to you. Even though she has no power here in the Dark Lands, I will respect her wishes."

"You're very generous. Where can we stay until tomorrow?"

The chief bellowed for one of his staff. "They will take you to where you will be comfortable for the night.

I expect you at first light, boy. Don't make me wait on you."

"Trust me, Chief Argus. I want to be done with this as much as you do. Good night. We'll see you tomorrow."

They were taken to a small, one-story cabin with a single window. They walked in, and Eleanor dropped their bag to the floor. The room had more space than the last hut he'd been in, and three beds lined the walls. They had the provisions Shayla and Cullin had supplied them with before they left.

Wayne pushed down on the mattress on the bed closest to the door and sat on it. "This bed feels comfortable, so I bet they're all in pretty good shape."

Eleanor chose the bed under the window. "I'll be glad when we conclude our business here. I've got some bad vibes from the tribe."

"We still have the return key if the situation gets out of hand." He walked over and sat next to her. "But I know it will all work out for the best. You'll just have to trust me on this."

"Still, I'll be happy to get back to Garland Falls even though the Dark Lands are my true home."

He walked to his bed and threw back the covers before getting under them. "Come on, gang. Let's get some rest. Tomorrow will be a busy day."

****

Wayne woke when someone shook his shoulder. He blinked the sleep from his eyes and looked up into the face of Odara. He sat up and grabbed the ogre woman in a fierce hug.

"Odara! I've been worried about you. The chief didn't take any action against you after my escape, did he?"

"No. He knows better than to make the one healer in the village angry. Now, come. Chief Argus waits for you at his home. He wants your companions to wait for you here."

Eleanor turned her eyeless gaze to him. "Will you be all right?"

He nodded. "I'll be fine. Argus and I will talk, nothing more. After that, we'll go home."

Wayne followed Odara to the chief's home. He took a deep breath and knocked on the door, then entered when told to do so. Today he would have a decent conversation with the chief. He crossed his fingers no one would lose their temper. At least he hoped that would be the case.

"Good morning, Chief Argus."

"Good morning, boy. Did you and your companions have a restful night?"

Wayne bowed. "Yes, we did, thank you." He hesitated and licked his lips. "Chief, you must let me apologize for my behavior the first time we met. I didn't want to hear what you had to say. I'm sorry I couldn't be more professional or more polite before."

Argus' eyes opened wide, and his mouth hung open. He didn't speak for several seconds while Wayne stared at him. "Apology accepted, boy. I guess I didn't behave very well myself. I insisted you bend to my will without any consideration of what you felt and how you viewed the tribe."

"Apology accepted." Wayne paused, not sure how Argus would take the next bit he wanted to say. "I also forgive you for when you withheld aid for my father. You had to do what you thought best to ensure the safety of the tribe. I think I was too hardheaded to actually listen to what you were telling me."

"I appreciate your forgiveness. For that, I give you my chief's blessing for you and your skeleton woman. She will make a strong companion for you." Argus sat in the chair behind him and held his head in his hands. "I'm sure you've found out how much politics rule everything here. I should've been stronger, should've defended him harder. I should never have let the former chief have his way."

Wayne walked over to him and rested his hand on the chief's shoulder. "I'm sure if you could've done more, you would have. It's all in the past. Let's let it stay there."

Argus lifted his head, and a ghost of a smile came out. "Agreed. Now, tell me how you can open the doors to this realm without a key."

"I don't know. After I came to Garland Falls, it happened all at once. I don't know if I'll be able to do it all the time or not. I thought maybe it has to do with both sides of my heritage and the fact it's close to St. Patick's Day in the mortal world. It could be my leprechaun powers are linked to that day."

Argus walked him over to a door. "Try, and let's see what happens."

Wayne concentrated on Dee's bed-and-breakfast. He touched the knob, and the door turned blue. He opened it and got hit in the face with snow. He slammed the door shut and wiped the flakes from his hair as they melted and the water dripped into his eyes. "I don't think the door opened where I wanted it to."

Argus laughed and thumped Wayne on the back, and he stumbled forward before he caught himself.

"You opened the door to the Winter Kingdom. Looks like you have the ability, but not the control. I believe control will come in time." He rubbed his chin as his gaze turned thoughtful. "Tell me, boy. Do you have any other relations in Garland Falls?"

"I don't think so, why?"

"It appears to me you might have a connection to the Keeper of the Keys. I believe she's away right now, but as soon as you can, try to meet with her."

"If you insist." Wayne glanced out the window and watched Eleanor and Hildegard talk with the ogres and Odara. "You should get to know Odara better. She'd be good for you."

The chief rubbed the back of his neck, and Wayne swore he saw the ogre's cheeks turn pink.

"Well, I have wanted to speak with her for some time."

"Do it. Maybe she'll mellow you out a little bit." He nudged the chief's shoulder. "I'm pretty sure she likes you. I expect to see the two of you as a couple next time I come back."

"You wish to return?"

"Of course. I want to know more about my family. I'd like to learn the ogre lore, and I bet you have some great tales to tell."

Argus rubbed his chin again. "Aye, that I do. I look forward to your return."

The chief opened the door, and they stepped outside.

Wayne waved to his friends before he turned back to Argus. "Does this mean we're free to go?"

"Yes, boy. It does. It's not good to keep family members prisoner."

Wayne looked at the ogre children as they played

and circled around Eleanor. "You know, chief, I'm looking forward to coming back. The children are a lot of fun to talk to, and as I said, I want to learn the lore." He reached into his pocket and pulled out more gold coins. "I'd like you to give the coins to the tribe. Maybe they'll give everyone a little bit of luck." He walked over to Eleanor and Hildegard. "Are you ready to hit the road?"

"Yes, Master Wayne, we are ready to return to where we belong."

The three of them walked to the edge of the village when Eleanor stopped them.

"We have the return key. Did you want to use it here, or do you want to use your newfound door-opening power?"

"As unpredictable as that particular power is? No, thank you. Use the key. I'm ready to be back in Garland Falls, and I'm tired of adventures for right now."

Eleanor walked to the nearest door, inserted the key into the lock, and knocked on the door three times. The door turned purple, and they walked through and into Miss Dee's backyard. As soon as they arrived, Eleanor became flesh and blood again and smiled at Wayne.

"I love seeing your eyes sparkle when you smile." He brushed her hair back, letting his fingers linger on her cheek. "Of course, I love your bony skull smile, too."

"Thanks." She looked at the lavender sky. "The sun has started to set here, but it looks like your rainbow followed you. Tomorrow, I have to get back to my store. I expect to see you there, bright and early."

"I'll be there before you open the door." He glanced down at Hildegard. "Will you stay here tonight, or do you want to go with Eleanor?"

"I'm here to serve you, Master Wayne. I shall tend to my duties at once."

Wayne took Eleanor's hand. "I'll drive you back to your place."

"No need." She squeezed his hand. "When we found out you were missing, I drove myself and Hildegard here. My car is parked out front. Besides, you've been through a lot more than I have. You should get some rest."

"I will, but only because you insist."

They walked to the bed-and-breakfast, Wayne with his arm around Eleanor's waist. As they turned the corner, they waved at Parker as he got ready to leave for the day.

"Parker, can you follow Eleanor back to her place? I want to make sure she gets home safe."

Parker looked at the three of them. "Where did you all come from?" He peered closer at Wayne's shirt. "And how did you come to wear the insignia of Queen Shayla?"

"It's a long story, and I'm too tired to tell you about it tonight."

Parker hesitated, then nodded. "Come on, Eleanor, I'll follow you home. Don't forget tomorrow's the St. Patrick's Day festival. You'll want to look your best. Mrs. Hall wouldn't have it any other way, and she'll expect you to be there."

Wayne waved as Parker and Eleanor drove down the hill. They had been in the Dark Lands longer than he'd thought. He didn't mention the rainbow. Could his friend still not see it? He stared at his hands. Maybe all his powers were stronger at this time of year. Maybe he could open the doors only at this time of year. At least

Chief Argus thought so. Once again, Garland Falls gave him too many questions and not enough answers.

"You know, my little town? If you want me to move here, I'd better start getting some answers out of you." A strong, quick breeze ruffled his hair. "I don't need a temper tantrum from you. Just answers." He smiled and glanced around him. "Good night, Garland Falls. I'm glad to be back here."

Chapter Twenty-Four

Wayne woke with the sunrise on St. Patrick's Day. He couldn't believe he could open his eyes as tired as he'd been the night before. He showered and spread some of the ointment Shayla had given him onto his feet. The soreness had eased, and the dull throb of the blisters had subsided to a slight ache.

He opened the door and inhaled. Miss Dee had made cinnamon rolls again. She must have known when he returned, and he didn't even question how she got her information. He hurried downstairs and into the dining room. Several other guests were there. Looked like she'd had some check-ins for the festival. No matter, as long as he got some breakfast and cinnamon rolls.

He filled a plate from the sideboard and listened to the others laugh and talk about what they would do when the festival started. He sipped his orange juice and tried hard not to smile. The whole scene looked so ordinary, but he knew he didn't fit the ordinary category any longer. If some of the tourists knew the secrets of Garland Falls, they'd be more surprised than he'd been when he found them out.

"Good morning, Wayne." Miss Dee plopped a plate of cinnamon rolls in front of him. "I'm glad to see you back safe and sound."

"Glad to be back, Miss Dee." He grabbed two rolls while she stood by. "How did you know when I'd been taken?"

"I haven't seen you for several days." She picked up the dirty plates and winked. "Did you have a good visit?"

"Well, parts of it weren't too great. Otherwise, it could be called good. Queen Shayla says hi by the way." When she smiled and walked to the kitchen, he followed her. "All right, Miss Dee. I know you know the ogres got in here and kidnapped me a couple of days ago."

She stacked the dishes in the sink and ran the water. "Yes, I knew. I also knew you needed to have the adventure in the Dark Lands. You learned so much more than you expected to, am I right?"

He caught the towel she tossed to him, a hint to dry the dishes. He waited while she washed some of the dishes, but she hummed a quiet tune and smiled. Would she tell him at least a couple of the secrets she held? He wanted to be patient but found it hard to wait. As he dried the dishes, she went back to the dining room for the rest. He held the door open after she bumped it with her hip.

As soon as they washed the dishes again, he had to start the conversation up. "Are you clairvoyant, or does your winter pixie powers give you some weird insight into what happens in Garland Falls?"

"It's a possibility. I've never questioned how I know what will happen. You see, Wayne, sometimes I know what needs to be done or what needs to be heard. I must keep it all to myself for fear it might change the outcome. Eleanor didn't let any harm happen to you, did she?"

"No, but I found out she's a skeleton."

Dee handed him a glass. "Her skeletal self comes out in the Dark Lands. After you saw her other side, did it change how you feel about her? A lot of us here can sense your emotions for her grow stronger every day."

"No. As a matter of fact, I felt closer to her. I mean, that isn't strange, is it?"

Dee chuckled. "Not at all. You're in Garland Falls. Love is all around you here. I know you have somewhere else you'd rather be. Go see your lady and tell Eleanor hello for me."

He kissed Miss Dee on the cheek and jogged to the front door. He needed to get to the bookstore where a beautiful skeleton—but not a skeleton in the mortal world—lady waited for him. He sped down the hill to Main Street and parked not too far from his destination. He ran to the bookstore and halted before he went in. He straightened his shirt and brushed his hair back.

He opened the door to the shop and waved to Eleanor as she helped a customer. When the customer left, he stepped up to the counter. "Hi. It looks like you've been busy today."

"I've had nonstop sales since I opened." She walked over to him and poked his chest lightly. "And you, sir, said you'd be here before I would open. I expect foot traffic to slow down once the parade starts."

"I'm sure it will." He leaned on the counter and gazed at her. "You want to go with me?"

"I'd love to. Oops, more customers coming in."

He glanced over his shoulder when the door chimed again. "I'll be back to get you. I have a few errands to run."

He hurried across the street to the empty store and took the number down. Of course, he'd move here. He might have fooled himself earlier, but no longer. He had Eleanor, his friends, and he couldn't forget Miss Dee's cinnamon rolls. He belonged in Garland Falls, and when he glanced up at the rainbow, it glowed the brightest he'd ever seen.

He took out his cell phone and called to make an appointment to get his paperwork filed. He knew his boss wouldn't be happy when he turned in his resignation, but the man would get over it. A lot of his co-workers coveted his position. He wouldn't have to take a lot of time to go back to Trenton to pack his stuff and turn in his apartment key.

He now had his business started, and he needed a home. He drove out to Callahan's Floral Emporium. The bell over the door dinged when he pushed it open.

"Hey, Wayne. Nice to see you back in town." Lucas leaned against the counter and folded his arms. "What brings you by today?"

"I wanted to see you before all the festivities start. When your assistant comes back from his honeymoon, would you tell him I'd like to buy his house?"

"So the town got to you, and you've decided to move here." Lucas narrowed his eyes as he looked at him. "It's not just the town either. You and Eleanor have fallen completely in love."

Wayne nodded. "We have. She knows all about me, and I've seen both sides of her. She's the one for me. How could I ever leave here, knowing I'd be leaving her, too?"

"I get it. My wife felt the same way. I told you Garland Falls has a way of getting to you."

"I'm glad it's a good way with people and not the creepy, horror-movie way."

"Agreed. Now go pick up your lady. The parade should be starting soon, and you'll want a good spot to see it."

Wayne drove to Main Street and had to park on the

next block over. He hurried to the bookstore and turned the closed sign over. He grabbed her hand, and she grinned as she trotted behind him to join the gathering crowd. He cajoled and shoved and got them a spot in front to see all the floats.

He squeezed her hand as she oohed and clapped when the parade marched by. "The floats are beautiful, but how about we make it more special? Watch this."

"How do you plan to do this?"

He winked and reached up to pull the rainbow down from the sky. It arced over the town with the end landing right on them. Who knew a man with a half ogre and half leprechaun heritage would fall for a skeleton woman who could also be flesh and blood?

He turned Eleanor to face him. "Looks like after I forgave my ogre family, my personal luck has changed to good." He kissed her and smiled when she kissed him back.

"The luck of the ogre/leprechaun has changed," she said as she touched her forehead against his. "And I like the new direction it's gone."

"Me, too, my beautiful bony love. Me, too."